Hippie Haven Homicide
A Psychedelic Spy Mystery
(*Book 2*)

by

Sally Carpenter

For information, visit our website at:
www.cozycatpress.com

COZY CAT
P R E S S

ISBN: 978-1-952579-04-2

Printed in the United States of America

10 9 8 7 6 5 4 3 2 1

Dedicated to all cat lovers and to my own cozy cats who inspired the character of Ceebee: P.K. Snuggles, Outdoor Kitty, Gabby, Felix and Boots

Author's Note

If you're new to the Psychedelic Spy series, this book is the sequel to the previous novel, *Flower Power Fatality*. Some issues from the first book are carried over into this one, so if something sounds unfamiliar, you may want to read *Flower* to see how the story began.

The 1960s were a time when religion, a mainstay of 1950s society, saw a massive upheaval: Vatican II for Catholics, and the rise of evangelicals, contemporary worship and the youth movement for Protestants.

Eastern religions made inroads into the Western world, most noticeably the International Society of Krishna Consciousness (ISKCON), popularly known as the Hare Krishnas, so-called because of their chanting. This group was the springboard for the sect SPARK—Spiritually Pure And Radiant Kin— that features in this book and clashes with the traditional values of the townspeople. I set up my own group so as not to offend anyone, although the ideology and lifestyle of SPARK was typical among the counterculture of the era.

The use of Noelle's cat, Ceebee, in spycraft was inspired by a real CIA program of the 1960s called Acoustic Kitty. Scientists tried to embed a microphone in a cat's collar so the feline could snoop on spies meeting in parks. Although the real project never got off the ground, the SIAMESE agents in this book make it work. When I researched the program, the story was too juicy to pass up. I'm sure you'll enjoy the spy work more than the cat did.

The character of Mamie Sprinkle was inspired by a real-life TV meteorologist: Marcia Yockey. At a time when female TV newscasters were rare,

Yockey reported the weather for 35 years, beginning in 1953, on WFIE-TV, Channel 14 (originally channel 62) in Evansville, Indiana. My family watched her broadcasts for years. You can find clips of Yockey and her unique style on YouTube.

Chapter 1: Feelin' Groovy
April, 1967
Monday

Police Chief Whitlock knocked the daisy from the hippie's outstretched hand. "Move along!"

A tear rolled down the young woman's cheek, smudging the bird painted on her skin. "Oh, bummer, man. Why did you smash my little flower? I was just giving you some love."

"I don't want your hippie love." Judd Whitlock put his chubby fists on his wide hips, which made his gut protrude even more beneath his black uniform and jacket. "Now you kids pack up your stuff." One hand made a sweeping gesture over the city park where they were standing. "And get out of town."

A young bearded man stepped up behind the girl. Both were in their early 20s and dressed in long-sleeved, ankle-length flowing blue robes with white rope belts tied around the waist. Both had brown sandals on their feet. They wore no coats, despite the April chill.

"Hey, Blossom, is this square making a bad scene?" the man asked.

"Yeah, Chakra," she replied. "All these bad vibes..."

The man put his hands on her shoulders as he eyed the cop. "Hey man, don't mess with Blossom's groove. I mean, she's just trying to lay down some love, and you're freaking her out."

The policeman crossed his arms. "Why don't you speak English?"

Chakra grinned. "Sure, man, we're picking up from where you're coming from."

"Then pick this up." Whitlock pulled a baton from his belt. The pair cringed and took a step back. "Now I want you freaks to leave now or—" He slapped the stick onto his palm.

Chakra looked at the girl. "We better blow this scene."

"We should fetch First Sage." She tossed back her waist-length black hair. "He'll know what to do."

"Yeah, that's cool." The man held up two fingers in a *V* sign at the cop. "Peace, man. We'll be right back."

The two beat a hasty retreat into the heart of Poinsettia Park, a large wooded community gathering place in downtown Yuletide, a rural town in southwestern Indiana. On weekdays, when school was in session, the large park was mostly empty save for a few housewives bringing their youngsters to play on the slides and swings, or retirees taking brisk walks and reminiscing about the good old days.

Today, however, about forty young adults, all clad in identical blue robes, scampered around the grassy area. They played tag; swung on the metal monkey bars; splashed in the fountain; made music with acoustic guitars and sang. Their laughter and music filled the air. All of the women—and the men too—sported long, free flowing hair. Most of the men were bearded as well.

The local folk who walked by gave the intruders the hairy eyeball and a wide berth.

"Judd, what the blazes is going on?" Christopher Kloss, the town's part-time mayor, puffed and panted as he jogged across the grass, which was still damp from the previous night's rain. "I came here as fast as I could." Like Whitlock, he too packed a few extra pounds, but for a good reason. The weight benefited Kloss' full-time job of portraying jolly old St. Nick at the Country Christmas Family Fun Park on the edge of town. The holiday theme park and the local electronics plant served as Yuletide's largest `employers.

Whitlock ran his eyes over the mayor. "Don't tell me you're going to give presents to the freaks?"

Indeed, Kloss was still clad in his red velvet Santa suit and hat, both trimmed with white fur. His natural white beard completed the costume. Kloss tucked his thumbs into his black leather belt. "You called me at work and said it was an emergency. I didn't take time to change. I came straight here. Now where's the emergency?"

"Here, Mr. Mayor." The chief pointed his baton at the clusters of young people scattered around. "These weirdoes have taken over the park."

Kloss' blue eyes squinted at Whitlock. "Who are they? They don't look like our usual type of tourists."

"I don't know. They drove into town in that."

The chief pointed the baton at a former school bus now painted orange with the words FOLLOW THE WISE ONE stenciled in black on the sides. Beneath that sentence, the phrase SPARK LOVE CAMPAIGN TOUR was painted in smaller letters.

"Who's the Wise One?" the mayor asked.

"I dunno."

"Why don't you find out?"

Whitlock wrinkled his nose. "I'd need to hose them down first to get close enough to ask. I don't think they bathe much."

Kloss chuckled. "Chief, have you ever been to a town hall meeting in a room full of farmers who've spent the day shoveling out their pig pens? They don't come in smelling like roses." He put a hand on Whitlock's shoulder. "Tell you what, Chief. You keep an eye on the kids, and if they cut down a tree or rob an old lady, you can arrest them."

"What if they start smoking marijuana?"

"Yes, definitely that. Otherwise, there's no law against adults having a good time in a public park. I'll go and see if I can find the person in charge."

The mayor headed toward the strangers. His shiny black leather boots made squishy noises in the damp grass. He approached a group of young men and women who were dancing around the city's war memorial, a tall stone pillar with the names of former Yuletide residents lost in the two World Wars.

A tall, lanky dude stopped and stared gaped-mouth at Kloss. "Hey, whoa, look out! It's the man with all the toys!"

His cohorts ceased dancing and began laughing. "Wow, man, where're your reindeer?"

"Are we at the North Pole?"

A teenage girl picked at the mayor's coat sleeve. "Cool threads. Where can I get one like this?"

Kloss yanked his arm away. "Please, don't touch. I just had this dry cleaned." He cleared his throat and spoke loudly. "Excuse me. I'd like to speak to the leader of your group."

"May I be of assistance?" A middle-aged man, older than the others, strolled up as if he wanted to take charge of the situation. His voice was quiet, but strong. Unlike the other men, he was clean shaven and wore his dark hair cut short. His robe was gold colored. Despite his average height and lean build, he radiated an air of authority.

"Yes, I'm the town mayor. Christopher Kloss. Are you in charge of these people?"

"I am known as First Sage."

"Do you have a real name?"

"That is the name that serves me well in my duties." He adjusted the wire-rim glasses on his long nose and ran his heavy-lidded eyes over Kloss.

"Don't mind my appearance," said the mayor. "I work at the local theme park. Who are these people, and what are your intentions here in our fair city?"

"Intentions? We have no intentions. Our only goal in life is to seek spiritual wisdom and be in harmony with ourselves and one another under the guidance of the Wise One." First Sage had a smooth, pleasant-sounding voice. "We are of the SPARK family: Spiritually Pure And Radiant Kin. Our cross-country Love Campaign seeks to spread our good news with others."

Kloss scrunched his lips and furrowed his brow as he tried to comprehend. "Are you a cult?"

The corners of First Sage's mouth bent slightly downward, displeased at hearing the question for the umpteenth time in his work. "We are a legally incorporated nonprofit organization that only seeks the betterment of mankind. Here, let the devotees tell you." He took one man by the arm and pulled him forward. "Chakra, tell the mayor about your life before you found us."

"I was lost, man. Strung out on booze, drugs—you name it, I did it. Sex—a different chick every night. But I wasn't happy. I was hurting and bummed out. Then I heard the Wise One speak at a rally and I said, 'Wow, now that's a bag I can groove with.' I joined the beautiful people, and I haven't shot up or gotten blitzed or looked at a girl since then. No way, man. I'm clean as a baby."

First Sage nodded. "He speaks for many of the devotees here. They were once lost, but now have found the way of beauty. Blossom, share your story."

The girl coyly glanced at the ground and clutched her hands together, then raised her eyes and smiled at Kloss. "I grew up in Homestead, Illinois. My home life was a bad scene. My daddy died soon after he remarried. My stepmom is a turn-off, and my stepbrother is a skuzz. But SPARK is the perfect family. Loving, caring, generous. I'm never going back to my old life. This is where I belong."

A clock, set at the top of the war memorial monument, struck noon with ear-splitting bongs.

"If you will pardon us," said First Sage, "it's time for the midday repast." He turned to face the blue-robed devotees. "Line up, children."

The members of the group clapped their hands and sang as they formed a line behind First Sage. They followed him, single file, to the side of the bus. Two male devotees stepped forward and lifted the door of the underneath cargo space. They pulled large boxes out of the space and set them on the ground. As the devotees walked by, the servers opened the boxes and handed them sandwiches wrapped in wax paper along with cardboard pint cartons of milk. The youth then scattered throughout the park in groups of six or more to eat. Since the ground was too wet for sitting, they perched on the playground equipment and the war statue.

First Sage returned to the mayor. "If you have no further questions, I have pressing business elsewhere. You may continue speaking with the children until they finish eating." He hurried to a white Cadillac that was parked near the bus. A male devotee was seated behind the wheel; he served as the chauffer for the group's leaders. After First Sage seated himself in the back seat, the devotee drove away via the service road that led out of the park.

Kloss peered over Chakra's shoulder. "What are you eating?"

Chakra held up his pita pocket sandwich. "Broccoli, chickpeas and avocado in lemon sauce! Yummy!"

Kloss' face turned ashen. "Ah, yes, very nice." He cleared his throat. "How can I meet this Wise Guy?"

"Who?"

"You know, the man in charge. The head of this, er, delegation."

"You mean the Wise One."

The devotees laughed.

"The Wise One arrives and leaves like the wind." Blossom was seated next to Chakra on one of the wooden benches. "He will come when he has more knowledge to impart to us."

Kloss jerked his head at the bus. "Didn't he ride in with you?"

"Oh, no," she said. "The Wise One uses his own transportation so he can meditate and ponder deep thoughts in solitude."

"And when do you all plan to return to your homes?"

"Never, man," said Chakra. "We'll ride the bus wherever it takes us."

"Umm, yes." Kloss glanced at the crowd of townspeople gathered at the park's edge. They were watching him and the devotees with keen interest. "Tell you what, please pass on a message to your Wise One. Tell him that I'd like to speak with him as soon as he shows up. In the meantime, you can stay in the park as long as you don't bother the residents. And when you finish, please clean up your trash, or you'll be on my naughty list."

As the mayor plodded away, the hippies regaled him with a chorus of "Here Comes Santa Claus." The next time the daffy police chief called him out for an emergency, Kloss would make it a priority to first change into his street clothes.

* * * * *

Noelle McNabb had been watching the gathering from the front window of the Groovy Vinyl Record Store, which was directly across from the park and on the other side of Kringle Avenue, the main street through town. She didn't hear what the people were saying, but she could tell something big was going on. Her part-time morning shift had ended at noon, and she was dying to go outside and check out the strangers. But first she had to wait for her customarily late afternoon replacement to arrive. She couldn't leave the store because of the one customer who was browsing the record bins. Noelle brushed some lint off her tan pants. She also wore a matching long-sleeved Mandarin collar shirt in a flower print. The customer finally came to the front counter to pay for his purchase: the newest singles by The Turtles, The Byrds and The Buckinghams. Noelle rang up the charges on the cash register with the mother-of-pearl keys, took the man's cash, and counted out the change. She wrote out a paper receipt for him and kept the carbon copy of the sale for the store. The last step was to place the vinyl discs into a flat paper sack printed with the store's name and logo. Shortly after the satisfied customer exited the front door—making the bell posted on the door frame ring—a friend of Noelle's slumped his way through the same door and into the building to work at the head shop in the back of the store. Noelle never stepped foot inside the head shop—that business was separate from the record store and nothing that concerned her.

Noelle had grown used to the man showing up for work in hippie time—that is, whenever he felt like it. "Hey, Rambler, what's up?"

The longhaired man waved and mumbled something under his moustache and beard. Today he had on a dirty Grateful Dead tee-shirt, torn jeans and a patchwork coat sewn from various fabrics and patterns.

"What's going on at the park, Rambler? Anyone you know?"

He peered through the window with his watery eyes. "Never set my peepers on them before."

"I thought you kept tabs on all the hippies in the area." She walked with him to the back of the store.

"Yeah, but these ain't hippies, just a bunch of religious freaks. They follow this cuckoo guru who calls himself the Wise One."

"What are they doing in Yuletide?"

"Sponging for handouts."

They stopped in front of the beaded curtain that covered the doorway to the head shop.
"Rambler, I'm off work now. I'm going to check out what's going on in the park."

"Groovy. And tell those cats to scoot. Don't need a bunch of flakes giving us real hippies a bad name."

He ducked through the beaded curtain, and Noelle chuckled. Most of the fair folks of Yuletide kept their distance from Rambler and his live-in girlfriend, Moonbaby, but Noelle found them to be loyal friends. She returned to the cash register to count the money in the till. The record store gig supplemented Noelle's principal work—playing the Winter Witch in the Candy Cane Capers show at the Christmas theme park—during the fall and winter months when the park was only open weekends. But the 25-year-old actress considered her park job to be temporary, just a step on her way to Hollywood fame and fortune.

At 12:15, the afternoon shift employee finally showed up and muttered some excuse about his tardiness. Noelle didn't listen. She slipped on her jacket, grabbed her purse, and ran outside, catching the stoplight in time to cross the street and dash into the park. The devotees had finished eating and were back to their playtime. Some of the youths stood in a circle and tossed a beach ball back and forth. When the ball went flying out of bounds, Noelle caught it before it sailed into the street.

She offered the ball to one of the girls in the circle. "Hi, my name's Noelle. What's yours?"

The devotee took the ball with her left hand. "The Wise One calls me Blossom. He says I'm like a flower planted in Mother Earth. The Wise One gave me the nutrients I needed to sprout into my true self, a self-actualized spirit capable of loving and being loved."

Noelle cocked her head, trying to absorb the reply. "What's your real name?"

"You mean the captive name that others called me when I was a slave to the material world? I no longer belong there."

"Yeah, that's telling them, baby!" Chakra, standing beside Blossom, gave her a playful punch in the arm.

"What about your family?" Noelle asked. "Don't you miss them?"

Blossom's smile sagged. Her voice lost its perkiness. "My material relatives are clouded by the vices of the world. My stepmother called me stupid. My stepbrother beat me. No, I don't miss them at all."

"Hey, Blossom, don't talk about them." Chakra rubbed her shoulders. "They're a bad trip. Think happy thoughts, like the Wise One says."

Noelle said, "I'm sorry you had an unpleasant childhood, Blossom. I'd miss my parents very much if I were away from them for a long time. I'd even miss my goofy siblings."

The smile returned to Blossom's face. "The Wise One is both father and mother to me."

"Where is he? I'd like to meet him."

Chakra grinned. "Hey, why don't you join us? You sound like a far-out chick."

"No thanks. I'm quite happy with my church," Noelle said. "I'm just interested in what other people think. So, what is it you do, besides play ball?"

Blossom replied, "Nothing. Wise One says we're his spiritual children, so we should play and be happy like little tots."

"How do you eat? Where do you get the money for the things you need?"

"The Wise One provides."

"Where does he get the money?"

The youths laughed. "All you think about is money," said Chakra. "You're just like all the other pagans."

Noelle stiffened. "Excuse me, I'm a Christian, not a pagan."

"Wise One says anyone not in the family is a pagan," he explained. "Pagans are obsessed with power and lust and greed. They can't see the way to true happiness."

"And you think happiness is tossing around a beach ball all day?" said Noelle. "What would happen if everyone did that? Who would grow the food and build the houses and keep the electricity and water flowing?"

The Cadillac pulled up beside the bus. First Sage got out of the back seat and marched over to the group with a clipboard in hand. "Listen, children, it's time for evangelism. Now that you have been fed with physical food, it's time to share our spiritual nourishment with others."

The devotees clapped and begin lining up behind First Sage.

He stared at Noelle. "Who are you? Someone with the mayor's office?"

"No, just a friend." Then Noelle turned to Blossom. "Can we maybe talk again later?"

"Sure." She took Noelle's hand. "You're friendly. I like you."

Noelle patted her hands. "I like you too."

First Sage frowned at Noelle. "The devotees have a full schedule of lectures and witnessing. They have no time for idle chatter with pagans." He grabbed Blossom's hand. "Come!"

He charged toward the bus with Blossom in tow. The girl twisted her head and, with her free hand, waved at Noelle, who returned the gesture. As the devotees climbed aboard the bus, First Sage returned to the car. The Caddy pulled away. The bus, with all the devotees aboard, followed the car out of the park.

Noelle put her hands on her hips and watched the group leave. She wasn't sure what to think. She liked Blossom, but wondered if she had fallen into the wrong bag. The 1960s had not only ushered in a new era of mod clothing, rock music and freedom, but had generated a revolt among the youth who questioned the principles of their parents. A plethora of new cults had popped up to attract the young people who were searching for answers. Had Blossom found a community of caring people, or had she been brainwashed by someone who sought to harm her? A strange feeling nagged at Noelle. She needed to keep an eye on the naïve devotee.

Chapter 2: I Call Your Name

But for now, Noelle didn't have time to ponder
Blossom's fate. She needed to pick up a few things
at the A&P grocery, and then rush home to set up for
a dinner and game night. Noelle's two jobs left her
limited time for socializing with her friends. Usually
Monday nights meant supper with her parents and
obnoxious younger siblings, but the twins had
suffered colds over the weekend, so Mrs. McNabb
had postponed the family dinner until Tuesday.
Noelle took advantage of the open date to invite her
friends to her place for food, snacks and a board
game.

After shopping, she drove her 1965 blue
Volkswagen Beetle to her rural, one-bedroom
cottage that was tucked back in the woods at the end
of a long gravel driveway off Ornament Lane. Once
inside, she turned up the thermostat, put away the
groceries, and tried to sweep the living room floor,
despite the distraction of her fat black cat, Ceebee.

"Hey! Will you get out of my way!" Noelle tried
to nudge Ceebee with the end of her straw broom.
"I'm going to sweep you up with the dust if you
don't move." The frisky cat wove around her legs
and fussed. "I fed you already, your highness."

Noelle took a step back, and her foot landed on
the cat's tail. Ceebee let out an ear-piecing yelp and
jumped on the couch.

"See? That's what happens when you bug me."
But she leaned the broom against the wall and sat
down on the sofa. Noelle put the feline on her lap
and petted him. "I'm sorry. I didn't hurt you, did I?"
The screeching subsided into a loud purr. Noelle
tried to stand up, but Ceebee remained on her lap,

wanting the attention to continue. "Look, I have to get ready for my guests. Can I get up?"

Noelle picked up the cat and set him on the sofa. Ceebee promptly jumped back on her lap. After a minute of this, Noelle found a ribbon bookmark on the cluttered coffee table and dangled it over the cat. Distracted, Ceebee swatted the toy long enough for Noelle to get on her feet and resume the cleaning. Ceebee tucked in his front paws and watched her from the sofa.

Noelle answered a knock on the front door. "Hi, Trevor. You're here early."

"I wanted to get a head start and avoid the school buses. They slow down traffic on the main streets." Trevor Spellman was a newspaper reporter and a bit of a rebel—he wore his red hair down to his collar and his sideburns long. He looked sharp in a plaid sport jacket, matching dark blue pants and a light blue shirt. "I can wait in my car."

"Nonsense, come on it. If you don't mind, you can help me set up."

"Be glad to help. Hello, Ceebee, you little cat burglar." Trevor gave the cat a pat on the head.

The two humans pushed back the furniture in the small living room and set up two cardboard-topped card tables, end to end. Noelle and Trevor were both 6-feet tall, so they saw eye-to-eye when they talked.

"So, Trevor, what did you find out about the park visitors?"

"What makes you think I know anything about that?"

"Because it's the most exciting thing that's happened in this burg since the murder case I solved." Noelle referred to the recent mysterious death of an out-of-towner.

"I helped you with that nasty business, didn't I?"

"Maybe a little." She set plastic placemats on the tables. "Besides, you can never pass up a scoop for the *Yuletide Herald*. Rambler says the newcomers follow some kind of guru. Are they the Hare Krishna people?"

Trevor set up folding chairs at the tables. "No, what we got here is a totally different group. This guru calls himself the Wise One. I've been following the guy. He's been making headlines across the country. His disciples live in St. Louis, at a huge estate some anonymous tycoon donated to them. SPARK also has branch offices in some of the big cities, including Indianapolis. When he's not in St. Louie, Wise One travels cross country on recruitment junkets to pick up fresh meat, which is what we have going on at the park. Wise One tells young people to quit their jobs, ditch school, and leave their homes to join him. His own version of 'turn on, tune in, drop out.'"

"But why? What does he get out of it?"

"Beats me. It can't be the money. The kids have nothing. Wise One covers all of their expenses—food, clothes, shelter, everything."

"Why haven't I heard of him?"

"This is his first trek through Southern Indiana."

They went into the kitchenette to set up bowls of potato chips and plates of cookies. Ceebee followed them, meowing pitifully until Noelle gave him a half-bowl of Purina Cat Chow.

"Did you meet Wise One?" she asked.

"No, he never showed up today. He travels separately from his followers. Apparently Wise One pops up now and then to give a pep talk and then disappears. His right-hand man, First Sage, runs the day-to-day operations. I managed to track him down on the street and speak with him a little. He didn't say much, except that they plan to stay in town for a week and hold a big rally."

"Doesn't sound like they're dangerous, just some peace-and-love beatniks."

"I don't know, Noelle. Some of these counterculture groups are fronts for the Commies or criminal activity." Trevor tapped a finger on the side of his nose. "My spidey-sense is tingly. Something's odd. How does Wise One pay for his organization? He sells a few books and cassette tapes of his lectures, and the kids pass the hat on the sidewalk, but that can't bring in much. As they say in the news trade, follow the money."

Noelle excused herself so she could change into something more fitting for a hostess. She closed the door of her bedroom and put on a blue-and-white checked A-line dress, nude pantyhose and white heels. She freshened her makeup, retouched her pink lipstick, and put on a delicate gold necklace with a large gold "N" initial. White plastic ball earrings peeked out from beneath the cheek curls of her short brown hair.

Their friends began to arrive, so Noelle and Trevor shifted the conversation away from the cult and onto less controversial topics. The guests parked their cars along the long gravel driveway that ran from two-lane Ornament Lane and ended at the detached one-car garage that housed Noelle's Bug. The guys wore casual shirts and pants; the gals were in shirtwaist dresses and slacks outfits. Noelle stored the various coats and jackets on her queen-sized, four-poster bed. After everyone had arrived, she heated up two large store-bought supreme pizzas and tossed a big bowl chopped lettuce, cut tomatoes, grated carrots and diced radishes for the salad. The women helped Noelle set up a buffet of paper plates, cups, bowls and napkins as well as plastic forks and straws, bottles of Thousand Island and ranch dressings, a bowl of ice cubes, a bottle opener and glass bottles of Coke on the kitchenette table. Noelle popped open a bottle of Frostie root beer for herself.

The crowd sat around the card tables with the food and drinks and dug in. Ceebee prowled beneath the tables so he could gobble up the fallen food scraps. Noelle finally picked up the chowhound and put him on an empty shelf on the bookcase.

The newly engaged Julia Beems was full of news about her summer wedding plans. Noelle suppressed her irritation at not having been asked to serve as an attendant. She and Julia had never been bosom buddies, but she had hoped this time she wouldn't be snubbed. Noelle had never been Miss Popular at Yuletide High School, and her peers rarely picked her as a bridesmaid. Weddings were big social functions in town, and taking part in one was an honor. Most of the brides recruited everyone they knew so they could fill up the church with a huge wedding party. Noelle was in no hurry to tie the knot herself, but despite her fierce independence she hated feeling like a social outcast.

When Julia paused long enough to take a breath, Noelle worked up the courage to speak. "Have you picked your bridesmaids yet?"

"Oh, sure. My older sister is my matron of honor, and my other sister is the maid of honor."

May Wells, a nurse with a towering beehive, said, "You can't do both a maid and a matron of honor. You can only have one or the other."

"I got two sisters. I can't leave one of them out."

Noelle persisted. "But what about the bridesmaids?"

Joe filled his plate with chips from the bowl. "Are we going to talk girl talk all night?"

"Say, Julia, where's your fiancée?" Trevor asked. "Why isn't he here?"

"He works the evening shift at the Penney's store." Julia talked around a mouthful of pizza. "But as soon we're married, he's pretty sure he'll be promoted to manager. Then he'll work days, and we'll have our evenings free."

The group finished eating, and Noelle cleared the tables. She brought out the Monopoly box, a favorite game, and set out the board, cards, paper money and tokens. Soon the friends were wheeling and dealing and buying up the properties and utilities. Julia, who could never balance her own checkbook, soon went bankrupt.

Noelle's token, the Scottie dog, had landed on a Community Chest square on the board when her turquoise Princess phone rang. Before she could get up to answer it, Trevor, who sat closest to the sofa end table, picked up the receiver.

"Hello?"

Trevor didn't recognize the male voice on the other end that said: "Fido Brown calling Tabby Gray."

"What?"

"Who is this?" said a strange voice.

"Sorry, bud," Trevor replied, "You've got the wrong number." He slammed down the phone.

"What was that all about?" said Noelle.

"A prank caller. Said he was Fido Brown and wanted to talk to someone called Tabby Gray. I guess he was trying to reach the dog pound."

The others laughed—but not Noelle. She lowered her face so nobody could see her cheeks burning red. She couldn't tell them that the caller headed a super-secret spy agency and was using their code names. He must want Noelle to join the agents for another important mission. But how could she return the call without raising suspicion among her friends?

Noelle coughed loudly. "Well, since Julia is bankrupt, we may as well call it a night."

"No way! The rest of us have plenty of dough." Joe reorganized his paper money. "Let's keep playing."

Noelle glanced at her Timex wristwatch. "Gosh, look at the time."

Joe snorted. "It's only 8:30."

"Yeah, but I've had a busy day, and I'm tired. I have to open the record store tomorrow."

"Noelle, the store doesn't open 'till ten," said Trevor.

May stood up and stretched her arms. "Turning in early sounds good to me. I'm on the morning shift at the hospital, so I should run along."

"Me, too," said Edna Apple, a teacher. "I have to set up my classroom before the kids arrive."

Luckily, for Noelle, with two players heading for the door, the others decided to depart as well. Some of the women offered to stay and help with the washing up, but Noelle shooed them away. She handed out the coats and jackets as quickly as possible. After what seemed like an eternity, the last car finally headed down the driveway to the main road. Noelle locked the front door, and quickly dialed a phone number.

"Tabby Gray calling Fido Brown. Is he there? He just called me. I can talk now."

A disinterested voice replied, "I'll give him the message," and ended the call.

The abrupt message system still rankled Noelle. For security reasons, Dash Hanover, the senior control operative of the Special Intelligence Apparatus for Midwest Enemy Surveillance and Espionage (SIAMESE), did not want her to call him directly. An operator passed on her messages for

Hanover to call her back. Noelle packaged up the Monopoly game pieces and had just placed the box on the closet shelf when the phone rang.

"Fido Brown. Where were you?" Hanover never wasted time with niceties.

"I'm sorry I couldn't take your call earlier," Noelle said. "I had friends over."

As usual, Hanover was curt and clipped. "If you're to be of any benefit to us, we must be able to reach you immediately at all times."

"What am I supposed to do, not have a social life like you?" As soon as she said the words, Noelle regretted her rashness. Dash made no reply, and the silence scared her. "I didn't mean to hurt your feelings."

"In my work, Miss McNabb, my feelings are not important. I work with my head, not my emotions. I suggest you do the same. SIAMESE has a new assignment for you."

Her pulse raced. She was flattered that he considered her worthy of another mission, despite the mistakes she'd made on her first job.

"What's up?"

"We've been following a surge of intelligence activity across the nation. Nothing major that would attract the attention of the CIA or FBI, but noticeable to us. A spy under the code name Old Scratch is selling prime government secrets to the enemy. He's also responsible for the expiration of two of our agents."

"Expiration?"

"He killed them."

Noelle gulped. Old Scratch sounded like someone she never wanted to meet. And how could Dash talk so coldly about death, as if the persons had just been tossed out like milk that had gone sour?

Hanover continued. "We believe the agent is in this area. He may be targeting one of the local electronics plants."

"You mean like Werner TecLab here in town? My father works there."

"Possibly. But Riverbend also contains a number of facilities that work with classified projects for the military. Tomorrow night I'll send around a car to pick you up and bring you to headquarters so we can discuss surveillance tactics."

"Great. I look forward to hearing about it."

"Do you still have a cat?"

The question took her off guard. "You mean Ceebee? What about him?"

"Bring him with you."

"Why?"

"We need him for the mission." The line went dead.

Noelle replaced the receiver and stared at the feline, snoozing in the bookcase. What on earth would SIAMESE want with her lazy cat? What kind of spying could he do?

Chapter 3: We'll Sing in the Sunshine
Tuesday

The next morning found shivering bodies strewn across downtown Yuletide. A light rain had fallen during the night, and the hippies had sought shelter under the roof of the bandstand in the park as well as in the doorways of the shops along Kringle Avenue. Wrapped in blankets, they huddled for warmth in clumps of twos and threes in the cool air. The police chief, however, was steaming mad as he strolled down the sidewalk.

"You can't sleep here." With the point of his baton, Whitlock nudged three young women camped in the doorway of the Groovy Vinyl store.

One girl, Morocco, yawned at him. "Is it morning?"

"Yes, and it's time for you all to be moving along."

"Yeah, but we got no particular place to go. We were just gonna hang out here and—"

"You're worse than the hobos. At least they stay out of everyone's way. Pretty soon the shops are going to open for business, and you can't be blocking the doors for the customers."

"So how are we going to catch some shuteye?"

One of the other girls said, "Hey, let's go stay at the fuzz's house! I call the sofa!"

They laughed until Whitlock gave them another poke with the baton. "Beat it before I arrest you for loitering and vagrancy."

"Hey, man, don't get uptight. Be cool." Morocco glanced at her blanket mates. "Come on, girls, let's bug out."

The scene was repeated several times as the cop roused the other sleepyheads clustered along the street. The hippies gathered under the roof of the bandstand, wrapped in their blankets and rubbing their arms. The

Cadillac drove up on the service road and parked beside the structure. First Sage, wearing a black raincoat over his robe, left the car and took a moment to survey the scene before he approached the police chief.

"Good morning, officer. Is there a problem?" he said.

"Who are you?"

"I am the First Sage, the chief counselor for the Wise One. I handle the daily care of the devotees."

"You're not taking very good care of them, letting them spend the night out in the rain. It's a wonder they're not all sick. And what kind of name is First Sage, anyhoo?"

First Sage lifted his chin. "A name that I am proud to bear. I am the first aide and confidant to the Wise One."

"Oh, a wise guy?"

First Sage merely glowered at the chief, not rising to the bait. "The children are sleeping under the stars because the hotels in this town refused to give us lodging. The managers said they were reserving their rooms for the tourists. Such is the prejudice we have frequently encountered during our travels. But, no matter. The children prefer to live close to nature."

"The nature along this street is off limits to them," said Whitlock. "We got laws about sleeping overnight on public property. They gotta go someplace else if they want to commune with the birds and the bees."

"Very well. I'll find more suitable housing," said First Sage. "But they can still use Poinsettia Park during regular daytime hours, correct? A public facility such as this lovely park should be open to all citizens."

"I suppose so, as long as they behave themselves. But I'm keeping an eye on them."

"They won't be any trouble. I can assure you of that. Now if you'll excuse me."

The chief grunted in annoyance. First Sage climbed the steps of the bandstand to speak with the devotees. The young ones smiled and clustered around him, like chicks flocking to their mother. After a brief check-in, the devotees happily followed First Sage to the bus, which they boarded. First Sage returned to his car, and the bus followed the Caddy out of the park. Whitlock hustled back to his patrol car and followed the caravan to see where the intruders would settle. They just might squat at The Star drive–in theater, which was closed for the winter.

* * * * *

After Noelle's morning shift ended at the record store, Trevor picked her up in his two-door Pontiac GTO coupe and headed for the local drive-in burger joint, In A Pickle. The weather was nippy for eating outside, but Trevor was in the mood for a hot lunch. He didn't want to spend time or money at the local sit-down restaurant, the North Pole Café, and the soda shop at The Igloo pharmacy only served cold sandwiches. In his black pants, a vee-neck green sweater and a white shirt, Trevor was warm enough to stay in the car and eat. Noelle, on the other hand, had a jacket buttoned over her cardigan sweater and blouse. Slacks, knee socks and low heels completed her outfit. She figured Trevor must be more hot-blooded than she was.

The In A Pickle waitress, who was shivering in her tights, shorts and long-sleeved uniform, brought their cheeseburgers, fries and shakes. She hooked the serving tray over the lowered windowpane on the driver's side.

Trevor took the tray, rolled up the window, and doled out the food.

He peeled back the wrapper on the steaming hot bun that held a beef patty, dressing, ketchup, mustard, cheese, lettuce, onions and pickles. "I had a busy morning at the downtown library in Riverbend. I went through the old newspapers on microfilm. Some of the big city papers have been writing about SPARK. So far, the group seems okay, nothing illegal or dangerous. Devotees are not allowed to smoke, drink, use drugs or have sex. Wise One doesn't appear to use his converts for prostitutes or criminal activity. The basic teachings are a little wacky, the usual love thy neighbor stuff mixed with astrology and Far East voodoo. Goofy, but mostly harmless."

She chewed on her cheeseburger. "When did you turn into a cynic?"

"I don't like shysters fleecing innocents in the name of God. According to the SPARK publicity machine, Wise One launched the group after he had a mystical experience and saw angels fighting demons."

"Maybe he did. I felt the Spirit at church camp when I committed my life to Christ. Not everything in life is fact and reason."

"That's what I like about you, Noelle. You keep me grounded." Trevor sipped the straw in his cup of Coca-Cola. "The Wise One, though, seems a bit slippery."

Noelle dipped the end of a French fry into a tiny paper cup of ketchup. "How so?"

"Nobody knows who he is, his real name or his past. SPARK has an official bio on him, but it's mostly fiction. He claims to have studied at the feet of the great Eastern mystics. My hunch is the closest he's ever been to India was listening to a Ravi Shankar record. Wise One popped up out of nowhere about five years ago, the same time that SPARK began. There's no record of him before then. What's he hiding?"

"Maybe he's on the lam but hiding in plain sight."

"Could be. A religious front is a pretty good cover. But if he's con artist, what's the payoff? His followers have no social status. He isn't schmoozing with politicians or celebrities. No one's found signs of embezzlement or a hidden Swiss bank account."

"So, what does all of this prove?"

Trevor sighed. "I don't know. Maybe nothing. Maybe the Wise One is really into peace and love and don't kick your dog. But if he pulls something funny in Yuletide, I'll spot it. Speaking of which, I better check in with the office and see what the hippies are up to. Are you done with your burger?"

Trevor gathered up the paper trash, left the car, and disposed of the refuse in a metal trash bin beside the restaurant's service window. Noelle remained in the car and finished her root beer float while Trevor called from the outdoor pay phone booth. When he hung up, he ran to the car and started the engine.

"The hippies have set up shop at the campgrounds. I need to check it out. Noelle, I'll drop you off at the record store."

"I'd like to come with you."

"You don't have to."

"I have nothing exciting planned for the afternoon, and I'd like to see Blossom again."

The GTO zoomed across town to Holiday Acres. During the summer, the grounds were packed with tourists and their aluminum campers. Church and youth groups throughout Southern Indiana rented the wooden lodges for their summer camps. But in the winter, Mr. Woodman, the manager who lived on site, only booked an occasional party or family reunion in the large dining hall on the otherwise deserted acreage.

By now the clouds had dissipated, and the sun shone brightly. The iron gates to the parking lot were open when Trevor pulled up. He bounded out of the car with pen and notebook in hand to track down Mr. Woodman for an interview. Meanwhile, Noelle headed for the cabins that sat atop a grassy hill where she found the devotees standing around First Sage. Noelle stayed out of sight to avoid a confrontation with the leader, who was reading the room assignments from a clipboard. The various cabins, each named for a different Indian tribe, were arranged in a horseshoe shape around the grassy area. Girls had the cabins on the east side; guys were in the lodges on west. In the "open" north area of the horseshoe stood a large facility that contained the kitchen, dining hall and meeting rooms. The restrooms, showers and laundry rooms were in the smaller buildings. Blossom and some of the other girls were assigned to the Shawnee Cabin. Noelle peered in the rear window of the cabin as the devotees entered through the front door. On the concrete floor of the square cabin stood three sets of bunk beds with footlockers at the end each bunk.

"I call a bottom bunk," said Blossom. "Heights make me queasy."

The girls quickly stored their meager belongings—socks, underwear, toiletries, sanitary supplies, wooden prayer beads and books written by the Wise One—into the footlockers. After Blossom put away her items, she straightened up and spotted Noelle, who motioned for her to come to her. Blossom glanced at her roommates. After they had all left the cabin, Blossom circled around the building and met Noelle behind the small structure.

Blossom seemed more shocked than pleased to see Noelle. "What are you doing here?"

"I came to see you."

"I can't talk with you. Last night, First Sage told us that we're not to speak to pagans unless we're witnessing to them."

"Witnessing?"

"When we're out in public and distributing our tracts. First Sage says the devotees have to stay together at all times to remain strong, and that the pagans want to lead us astray."

"Blossom, are you really happy here?"

"Well, yes, of course."

"You don't sound like it. Is something wrong? Are you being held against your will?"

"Of course not. I chose to follow the Wise One. He only seeks our happiness. My pagan family is begging me to come back, but they're mired in the ways of the flesh."

"If you ever feel this isn't right, I have friends who can help you."

Blossom's eyes blazed and she stepped back. "You're a demon tempting me back into the material world!"

"No, no, Blossom. I like you. I really do. I don't want to see you hurt. Is everyone treating you all right?"

"Yes, yes, of course, except for—"

"Yes?"

Blossom lowered her face. "Never mind. It is not worth discussing."

"What? Did someone hurt you?"

"It was my fault. I should not have snooped into things that are forbidden for me to see."

"What happened?"

From across the yard a whistle blew, followed by a loud shout from First Sage. "Children! Come gather!"

"I really must go," Blossom said.

Noelle grabbed the girl's shoulder. "Tell me what happened!"

Blossom pulled away and ran across the lawn. She joined the others as they formed a line and, clapping and singing, entered the dining hall for their lunch. A smile returned to Blossom's face—but was the grin real or pretend? Noelle couldn't tell. She returned to the GTO. Did she have any right to urge Blossom to leave the cult? Maybe the girl had indeed found a happy place. But if so, why was she scared?

Chapter 4: A Day in the Life

Trevor met up with Noelle at the coupe. "I hope your investigation was more successful than mine."

"Not really," said Noelle. "Now I have more questions than answers."

"Same here."

On the drive back into town, Trevor shared his interview with Mr. Woodman. The manager didn't like First Sage, but Holiday Acres was empty, and Mr. Woodman needed the extra income. First Sage leased the entire campgrounds for a week and paid in cash—no check or credit card to trace.

"Obviously the group is traveling with a good deal of money," said Trevor. "They're lucky nobody has robbed them. Taking over the entire campgrounds must have cost a bundle. Mr. Woodman said the group wanted other campers off the grounds so they could have peace and quiet, but I think they don't want anyone spying on them. Mr. Woodman said he hasn't seen the Wise One yet. I left word for him to call me right away if the guy shows up. I'm beginning to think that the Wise One doesn't exist. He's a smoke screen, like the Wizard of Oz. Maybe First Sage is really the brains behind the outfit."

Trevor drove west on Kringle Avenue. "You know, Noelle, I can see how the SPARK lifestyle attracts people. No jobs, no work, no responsibilities, just fun, fun, fun. First Sage calls them children and that's how they behave, like innocent kids, with Big Daddy protecting them against people like us."

"I don't think the devotees are doing anything wrong," said Noelle. "They're just looking for friends and love. Aren't we all?"

"Me? I'm out for that big scoop that's going to launch me to a big city paper."

"Come on, Trevor. What happens when that happens? You'll be in Chicago with no more worlds to conquer. Will you be happy then?"

"Don't get righteous on me, sister. You're the one who's pining for that star on the Hollywood Walk of Fame."

"Touché. You got me there. But I don't intend to lose my morals along the way."

"Fair enough." Trevor swung the GTO into the parking lot behind the record store and pulled into the spot next to Noelle's car. He let the car idle in park. "Here's your stop, madam."

"Gosh, Trevor, I didn't get a chance to tell you about Blossom."

"You spoke with her?"

"Barely. She was in a hurry to get away from me. First Sage had told the kids not to talk with outsiders. She seemed upset about something, but wouldn't tell me what."

"Well! Maybe something shady is going on after all. But I'll have to look into it tomorrow. If there's a juicy story, it'll take some time to dig it out, especially if nobody's talking."

Noelle thanked him for the ride and got out of the car. As the GTO sped off, the clock in the park bonged the hour. Noelle needed to rush across town to make her dinner date with her family. She didn't have time to run home, change clothes and feed the cat. At the McNabb home, dinnertime was held promptly the same time every weekday, shortly after Mr. McNabb arrived home from work. Noelle sped to her parents' house on Reindeer Road. Generally, she arrived early enough to help Mom with the preparations, but today the table was set and her father was already home from work.

"Sorry I'm late." Noelle striped off her jacket and hung it in the coat closet beside the front door. Dinner simmered on the stove and filled the air with the rich aroma of beef stew with thick chucks of meat and fresh carrots, potatoes and peas in brown gravy.

"I was getting worried." Mom ladled the stew into a china serving bowl and placed it on a ceramic hot plate in the center of the Formica-topped dining room table. "I was ready to call to see if you weren't coming."

"I was out at the campgrounds with Trevor, talking to the SPARK devotees."

"Why would you want to do that?" Dad entered the dining room. He'd removed his tie but still wore his long-sleeved white shirt and brown work pants. "They look like a bunch of oddballs, if you ask me."

"They aren't so bad, once you get to know them." Noelle leaned over the table and sniffed the still-bubbling stew. "A little misguided, but they're okay."

"But do they believe in God?" Mom asked.

"I don't know," Noelle said. "I didn't ask."

"What is it with the young people today?" Dad asked. "My generation worked hard to build good cities and to raise families. Today we get loafers in robes who hang around the park and do nothing all day."

"I'm sure they're happy at what they do," said Noelle."

"Doing an honest day's work for a day's pay is rewarding in itself," he replied.

"My generation sees things a little differently."

"Yes, but you're a hard worker. You don't go begging on the streets for money. No child of mine is lazy."

Mom placed a platter of homemade bread, cut into thick slices, and a plate of butter pats on the table. "Your father and I have to eat quickly. We're going to the emergency town hall meeting tonight at the high school auditorium."

"What meeting?" said Noelle. "I didn't hear about it."

"I found out through the phone tree." Mom referred to the system whereby the ladies of the town called certain people to speed along messages. "Everyone's concerned about what to do with the strangers. They're a nuisance. I was on my way out of the grocery store today, and one of them shoved a brochure into my hand. He wouldn't let me pass unless I gave him some money. And Mabel," the town gossip, "told me that at the high school, the hippies were asking the kids to leave home and join them!"

Dad shook his head. "It's a sad day when the women and children of this town can't walk down the street without being accosted."

Noelle said, "I'd like to go this meeting myself and see what's up."

"No, dear," Mom said. "Father and I were hoping you'd stay here and watch the kids. I called the babysitters, but they all have homework tonight."

"But, Mom, I have plans—" Noelle stopped. She couldn't tell her folks that she had an appointment with a spy agency. "I need to go home and feed Ceebee."

"Oh, that cat's fat enough. He'll last another hour or two," said Mother.

"The meeting shouldn't last long," said Dad. "A few people will air their gripes, and the council will look over the city laws to see what they can do. The mayor doesn't like to let these special meetings run too long."

Mom brought in a tray with small plates, each with a cube of Jell-O with fruit inside. After setting a plate at each setting, Mom removed the apron that covered her blue dress. "Noelle, will you call the twins?"

Inwardly the daughter groaned, but she ran to the stairs anyway. Her brother and sister were eight years old, which meant they were too young to be good companions with Noelle. Her siblings' childish interests bored her. When Noelle was old enough to go out with her friends, she was often stuck at home, babysitting— just like tonight.

From the base of the stairs, she yelled, "Donny! Dolly! Time for supper!"

"Dear, don't shout," said her mother. "Go upstairs and fetch them."

"They should know it's time for supper," said Noelle. "Happens the same time every night."

Noelle skipped up the stairs, two steps at a time. On the second floor she spied inside the open doors of each twin's bedroom. Dolly, dressed in a playsuit, was sprawled atop her twin bed, engrossed in the latest issue of *Tiger Beat* magazine. In Donny's room, the boy, in a plaid shirt and dark pants, was at his desk carefully fitting together the plastic pieces from a model kit of the USS Enterprise spaceship.

"Donny!" Noelle called. "Time for supper!"

"Ah geez!" he replied. "I can't go. I gotta hold this together until the glue dries!"

"Dolly!"

"In a minute! I just started this groovy article about Davy Jones!"

Before Noelle retreated to the kitchen, she gave a final warning. "Don't make Mom come up here and get you two."

She hurried downstairs to where her parents waited. "I delivered the message, but it was not received.

Dolly's reading one of those stupid teen mags, and Donny's building something or the other."

"It's good the kids have hobbies to occupy their time," Dad said.

"They should be doing their homework," Mom replied. "Donny has his mind in the clouds along with his spaceships, and he won't pay attention in class. His teacher is very concerned."

"I'll have a talk with the boy."

The pounding of feet on the stairs announced the arrival of the younger siblings. They pulled out their chairs at the table and began to sit down.

"Wash!" Mother ordered.

With much grumbling the twins headed into the sole bathroom and fought over the soap bar.

"Was I that much of a pain when I was their age?" Noelle asked.

"There was only one of you, so that much was easier," Mom said, "but you had your cranks as well. Incidentally, I don't recall seeing you wash your hands after you came in."

Noelle trudged to the kitchen sink to soap up.

At last, the family was clean and seated at the table. They folded their hands and bowed their hands as Dad said grace, then Mom ladled stew into the bowls and passed around the bread plate. Dolly kicked off the conversation with a tale of what the mean girl at school did during recess. Mom told her to never act that way herself. Donny wanted an increase in his allowance so he could buy another model kit, a Klingon war ship, but Dad said no, he'd just have to save his pennies. After everyone had polished off the stew and Jell-O, Mom brought out a homemade chocolate layer cake and cut slices for the dessert plates. The tykes finished eating and were excused, then rushed into the living room to watch *The Girl From UNCLE* on TV. Noelle longed to tell them that the show bore no resemblance to her experiences working with real-life spies.

With the kids out of the way, the talk returned to the city visitors.

"How long are these hippies going to stay in town?" Dad asked.

"Trevor told me they rented the lodges at Holiday Acres for a week," said Noelle.

"Really? I thought they were just passing through."

"I think they should move on," said Mom. "They're disrupting everything. If they keep bothering people on the sidewalks, they'll scare away the tourists. You wouldn't want the park to close, would you, Noelle?"

To avoid answering, Noelle ducked her head and forked a big chunk of cake into her mouth. Having grown up in Yuletide, the park was no big deal to her. The silly musical show that she appeared in meant nothing more to her than a way to earn money for her move to Hollywood and a real acting career.

"I think you're being harsh on them, Mom. Just because the devotees are a little different doesn't mean they're bad people."

"They're so strange," Mom said. "Wearing robes in this kind of weather. And they're a bad influence on the youth. The parents in this town work hard to instill good values in their kids. We don't want our city to become run down and crime-ridden like Riverbend."

"I think we should get to know them better before we jump to conclusions." The discussion was going nowhere, so Noelle changed the subject. "How are things going at the plant, Dad?"

He looked up from his dessert plate, startled. "Fine, I guess."

"Any new projects you're working on?"

"You know I can't talk about that. We've been involved in some top-secret assignments for NASA."

"Seems odd that the government would send a big project to a little podunk town."

"The rockets are built in the big factories. The small electronics work is spread throughout the country."

"Have any of these small plants been hit with break-ins or thefts?" In a covert way she was trying to find out if Dash Hanover was right about spy activity happening in places like her father's workplace.

"I wouldn't know what goes on at the other facilities. Why do you ask? We have pretty good security at TecLab."

Mom wiped her mouth with her napkin and stood up. "Noelle, would you please be a dear and clear the table? Your father and I need to leave."

"All right," she replied. "I just hope the town council doesn't do anything drastic. You know how hot-headed some of these farmers can get."

Dad rose from his chair. "Don't worry, Noelle. We won't tar and feather the intruders."

Noelle loaded up the dirty dishes into her arms and carried them into the kitchen as her parents put on their coats. She wasn't pleased about missing her appointment with SIAMESE, but what could she do? She couldn't call Dash about the delay. Hanover had rigged the Princess phone in her cottage with an anti-eavesdropping device, but she couldn't make secured calls from her parents' phone. And dragging the twins along to her appointment was out of the question. Noelle was stuck on Reindeer Road, incommunicado.

After her parents left, she washed the dishes for something to do. During the TV commercial break, the twins rushed into the kitchen, clamoring for cookies and glasses of Kool-Aid. She fed them just to shut up them up. When the TV show ended, Noelle urged them to go upstairs and do their homework, but the tykes insisted on watching *The Red Skelton Show* instead. So, Noelle sat in the living room with the kids, chuckling at the funny man's sketches. She liked Red because he was a native Hoosier too, born in Vincennes, Indiana. The twins sat still, eyes glued on the boob tube and not hassling their big sister. How did parents manage their kids before the electronic babysitter was invented?

An hour later, after Red had ended his show with his customary, "Good night, and God bless," her parents came home. Noelle was dying to know the outcome of the meeting, but she didn't have time to chat. As soon as Mom opened the front door, Noelle sprang to her feet, gave each parent a quick goodbye kiss, and swore that the twins had behaved. She grabbed her jacket out of the closet and dashed to the Bug. She switched on the headlights and sped home through the night, wondering how badly Hanover would chew her out for her tardiness. But he had to understand that she wasn't a full-time agent with SIAMESE. In fact, she didn't have to work for them at all. She wasn't ready to give up her home and social life—such as it was—to spend her time snooping in dark alleys.

But when she arrived home, the gravel driveway leading to her cottage was empty of other cars. Hanover must have grown tired of waiting and left. She sighed in relief. With her jobs and the devotees in town, she had plenty to juggle without a spy mission. Noelle stopped the car and got out to open the garage door. Soon the car was tucked away for the night and Noelle was on the walkway that led to her front porch. A famished

Ceebee ran in from the surrounding woods and danced at her feet. Noelle stuck her key into the front door, but it swung open with no effort. How strange. She was always careful to lock the door whenever she left. The living room light was on too. Noelle worried. She distinctly remembered shutting off the lights earlier; she was prudent not to waste electricity and to keep her utility bills affordable. Noelle cracked opened the door and peered inside.

A stranger was sitting in her recliner chair and watching the door.

Chapter 5: Leave My Kitten Alone

The intruder wore a nice brown coat with brown dress slacks. His dark hair was short and styled. His face was clean shaven and unremarkable. He wasn't a tramp looking for a handout.

"Miss McNabb?" His voice was all business.

She remained on the porch. "You broke into my house. Get out!"

"Don't worry. Your door locks are undamaged, although they are extremely easy to pick. I recommend you purchase some sturdy deadlocks for your home."

"I'm going to get the police!"

"I'm here to take you to SIAMESE headquarters." The man stood up, removed a wallet from an inside coat pocket, and held it out for her to read. The billfold contained a SIAMESE identification card with his thumbprint and photo embedded in the plastic card. Noelle was a little relieved that he wasn't a crook, yet annoyed at how the brassy SIAMESE agents felt they could just pop into her home without an invitation.

"I was expecting Dash Hanover," she said.

He returned the wallet to his pocket. "The senior control operative is too busy with other duties to run a simple pick-up assignment. He will meet you in the briefing room at headquarters."

"How did you get here? Nobody tailed me from town."

"My car is parked behind the garage, out of sight of your landlords. I've been here for some time. Don't worry; I didn't search your drawers or read your mail." Good heavens, the guy even talked like Hanover. Were all SIAMESE agents so drab and soulless?

He glanced at her feet. "Is that your cat?"

Around her ankles, Ceebee was making his frantic feed-me-now-or-I'll-die dance on his back legs, along with his accompanying wail of pity.

"Yeah. Mr. Hanover said something about Ceebee. Why on earth does he want my cat?"

"I don't know. I haven't been briefed on your mission."

"He's hungry. I have to feed him first before we go, Mr.—what's your name?"

"You don't need to know. And we need to leave now."

"Ceebee's gonna raise a stink if he isn't fed." The man glared at Noelle. "Okay, I'll just get the carrier, if that's all right with you. Excuse me."

Why was she asking permission to move around inside her house? Noelle set her purse on the living room table, and removed the metal cat carrier from the floor of the closet. She set the box on its end on the kitchenette table and opened the carrier's wire door on the top end. The best approach to caging a reluctant Ceebee was to drop the cat into the box, using the force of gravity to get him in. Ceebee had followed her into the kitchenette, thinking he was getting food, but at the sight of the carrier he howled and ducked under the living room sofa. Noelle knelt on the floor, lifted the dust ruffle of the couch, and tried to coax out the cat. She glanced up at the man, who stood over her and watched intently.

"Sorry," she said. "This may take a while."

"We haven't got a while."

"I can tell you don't have pets."

She retrieved the broom from the hall closet. The man opened the face of his wristwatch, unspooled a wire that contained a receiver piece on the end, stuck the device into one ear, and spoke a coded message to SIAMESE headquarters on his watch radio. No doubt he was telling Dash that they were running late due to a stubborn cat. As he talked, Noelle gently poked the broom under the sofa. Ceebee ran out from his hiding place and clawed on the back door. Noelle grabbed the cat around his fat middle and lifted. The feline squirmed and fussed. She attempted to drop the cat into the carrier, but his paws gripped the sides of the opening.

She looked at the agent sheepishly. "If you're finished with your conversation, can you help, please?"

The man eyed her, then signed off his message and removed the earpiece. He restored his watch as it was and stepped into the kitchenette, eyeing the cat with trepidation.

"If you would hold the carrier," she said. "Ceebee likes to knock it off the table."

The agent gripped the sides of the crate, keeping his hands away from the cat. A hard-core veteran agent terrified of a house cat. Noelle managed to pry Ceebee's claws off the box and shove the cat inside. She quickly shut the carrier door and latched it. Ceebee shrieked.

"Is the cat injured?" the man asked.

"No, he's fine. He's a pest about being cooped up. I can't imagine why Hanover wants a cat, unless he plans on using Ceebee to claw out the eyes of an enemy spy."

With the carrier in one hand and her purse in other—Noelle still had her jacket on—she followed the man out of the house and locked the door behind them. As he said, a black SIAMESE company car was parked behind the garage. The agent opened the back door for Noelle to get in, and soon he was driving them down the road. Due to the tinted windows, Noelle couldn't see the route to headquarters—for her protection, she'd been told before. She'd given up trying to figure out the various turns and stops of their trip. For all she knew,

SIAMESE was probably in a cornfield just down the road from her house. A dark Plexiglas barrier was in place on the back on the front seat, making conversation impossible between her and the driver. At least he didn't have to listen to Ceebee yowling from inside the carrier. Noelle settled back into the plush leather seat and tried to comfort the cat to no avail.

A sudden drop down a steep ramp indicated they'd entered the SIAMESE underground facility. The car descended into the parking area full of other company cars. From there, the agent and Noelle, with carrier in hand, walked to the security checkpoint where the agent passed both a fingerprint and eye retina scan. He punched the passcode into a keypad, and a door slid open. Inside the entryway, Noelle hung up her jacket in a closet as the agent removed two security badges from the hooks on the wall. He took a red field agent badge for himself and handed Noelle a yellow visitor's badge. All the security badges were hung on long black lanyards.

She smiled as she slipped the lanyard around her neck. "Does my cat get a security badge too?"

"Indeed, he does."

"I was joking."

"I wasn't."

From another wall hook the agent removed a black elastic cat collar; a tiny yellow badge dangled from a metal ring. Noelle set the carrier on a shelf and carefully opened the box. Instead of springing out, Ceebee huddled into a corner, wary of the new environment. Noelle reached into the crate and slipped the collar around the cat's bare neck.

"Look at you, Ceebee!" she said. "Now you're an agent too." She closed the carrier and grinned at the man. "Ceebee is very good at keeping secrets."

The agent said nothing. He pushed a button on the door, and they entered the heart of SIAMESE operations. They passed through a sterile metal corridor and stopped in front of a door that automatically slid opened with a soft whoosh. The man held out his hand, indicating that Noelle should go inside. As she did so, he proceeded down the hall to his next assignment. The door closed behind Noelle. A long table surrounded by metal-and-leather chairs filled most of the sparsely furnished briefing room. Dash Hanover stood at the far end of the table. He hadn't changed since the last time Noelle had seen him: same drab suit and tie, same purple badge, same buzz haircut, same piercing brown eyes, same rigid posture—but did she detect a touch of gray in his dark hair?

He frowned. "You're late. Our time is valuable."

"I'm sorry." She set the carrier on the table. "My parents roped me into a last-minute babysitting job. I couldn't very well tell them I had a spy mission planned."

"Apparently we'll need to provide you with a radio so you can contact us during emergencies."

"All right. I'm here now. What's up?"

The hall door whooshed open again. A tall black woman in a short afro entered the room. A red field agent's badge dangled around her neck. She moved across the carpet as gracefully and quietly as a cat. She looked stunning in a purple jumpsuit, black ankle boots and belt, and large gold hoop earrings. The agent always wore such fab clothes.

Noelle said, "Hello, Destiny! Great to see you. Nobody told me I'd be working with you again."

The woman gave a wry smile. "Noelle. What's happening?" She held out her palm and Noelle gave it a gentle slap. Destiny King, in returned, slipped her some skin as well.

Ceebee howled and banged against the metal walls of his cage.

Noelle blushed. "Can I let my cat out before he hurts himself?"

Hanover nodded. Noelle opened the crate door. The cat slinked out, his big yellow eyes surveying the strange surroundings. He sniffed the air and padded across the table toward the two spies. Ceebee growled at Dash, who didn't react.

"Sorry about that," said Noelle. "Ceebee, be nice to the man."

The cat moved across the table until he was in front of Destiny. He stopped and purred. The corners of Destiny's mouth twitched up as she petted the cat.

Hanover stared at her. "Miss King, your aptitude tests never indicated a particular fondness for animals."

Destiny jerked her hands away from the cat. The brief sparkle left her dark eyes. "Don't worry, sir. It won't distract me from the mission."

For a split-second Noelle thought she caught a glimpse of pity in Hanover's eyes as he studied Destiny. Or maybe not. Noelle marveled at how the agents hid their emotions, as if turning off a faucet in their hearts.

"Yes, the mission." Hanover was all business once again. "Take a seat, ladies."

Hanover sat at the head of the table with Destiny on his right. Noelle remained at the far end of the table and called to Ceebee. The cat hurried down the table and jumped into his familiar master's arms. Noelle took a chair and put the feline on her lap. The women turned their attention to Hanover.

"We've had a difficult time tracking Old Scratch because we don't have a name or photograph of him," said the chief. "But we have reason to believe he's in the area. We need to conduct surveillance and discover his plans."

"You said he was after the tech labs," said Noelle. "Do you want me to go undercover at the Yuletide plant?"

"Impossible. Too many people know you. I doubt that you could fool your neighbors, even with your superb acting skills. No, what we need are ears. We have a reliable report that Old Scratch plans to meet with an unfriendly agent tomorrow in a park in Riverbend. We need to listen in on that conversation."

"If they're outside," said Noelle, "that should be easy."

"On the contrary. Old Scratch won't talk if he sees someone lurking nearby. The contact might also recognize one of our agents. He'll no doubt scan Old Scratch for bugs before they talk, so we can't plant a listening device. A long-range audio scanner would pick up street traffic."

"So what you do want me to do?" Noelle asked.

"Not what *you* can do. Your cat. Nobody would suspect a stray animal walking by in a park."

"You mean, use Ceebee for surveillance?" asked Noelle.

"Just what kind of a name is Ceebee?"

"Short for cat burglar. He likes to steal stuff."

Destiny said softly, "Sounds like he'll fit right in with what we do."

Hanover gave Destiny a glance, then continued. "Our scientists have created a cat collar with a miniature microphone embedded in it. The mic can pick up sound from within several yards. If your cat can get close to the enemy, we can record vital information."

"Ceebee doesn't like wearing collars," Noelle said. Indeed, the feline was scratching at his badge with his back paw and growling.

"He won't have it on for long, just for the mission. Miss McNabb, can we count on your cooperation?"

"I'm willing. I'm just not sure about Ceebee. How much time does he have to get used to this collar?"

"Very little," said Hanover. "We have to move now."

"You folks don't plan ahead, do you?"

"That's the nature of our work. We can't predict when the enemy will move. If you're ready, follow me to the lab."

Hanover headed for the hall door. Noelle scooped up the cat in her arms; attempting to reinsert him into the carrier would be a lost cause. With her hands full, Noelle caught Destiny's eye and nodded at the carrier. The black woman grabbed the handle of the empty crate. The women followed Hanover out the door and down the long, drab hall. The pumped-in air was cold, and Noelle regretted leaving her jacket behind at the entrance. The trio entered an elevator at the end of the hallway. The senior operative pushed a button and the cab plunged several floors.

"Just how far are we going?" Noelle asked.

"The lab is on the bottom level," he said.

As the cab moved, Noelle tried some small talk to ease the silence. "Destiny, what have you been doing since I last saw you?"

"Our missions are classified," she replied.

"You don't have to give me details, just a hint. Your work is so fascinating."

Destiny glanced at Hanover; he nodded his approval. She said, "I prevented the assassination of a major American government official; stopped the devaluation of the American dollar; retrieved stolen documents; and prevented the kidnapping of the child of a top government official."

"Wow! You did all that in one week?"

Destiny shrugged. "I'd hate a job where I was stuck in a rut."

The cab lurched to a halt and the door opened. Ceebee began to whine. The agents stared at the cat.

Noelle smiled sheepishly. "Ceebee didn't get his evening meal. Your guy rushed me here before I could feed him."

Hanover gave her the ugly eye, then led the women down yet another long, plain hallway.

Noelle muttered to Destiny, "Cats will be cats."

"Yeah, but when it's a SIAMESE cat, he's gotta dance to Hanover's tune," the spy replied.

They entered a room lined with shelves stocked with boxes, jars, scientific reference books and notebooks full of experiment notes. The tables stuffed into the small space were covered with microscopes, Bunsen burners, tubes, beakers, jars of chemicals and various electrical and mechanical devices. A man in a white lab coat and dark trousers waited for them beside the large center island. His white hair stuck up comically, as if he were amused to see them. His wrinkled face belied his age. His thick bifocals made his blue eyes look even larger. Around his neck hung the security badge—with black and white diagonal stripes—of the internal support staff, those who remained inside headquarters to equip the outside field agents.

"You must be Noelle. I'm Dr. Albedo. We're glad to have you working with us." Unlike Hanover, his voice was warm and friendly, and contained a tinge of an east European accent. But Noelle couldn't see his lips move beneath his bushy white moustache.

"This is one of our veteran scientists at SIAMESE," Dash said.

"Please put your animal on the counter." Dr. Albedo patted the metal-lined top of the island.

Noelle placed the cat on the spot. "You wouldn't happen to have any cat food, would you? Ceebee is starving."

"It's good that the cat hasn't eaten. It's best for animals to fast before surgery."

"Surgery!" Noelle scooped up Ceebee. "No way are you cutting into my pet!"

"We need to implant an earpiece for the animal. Otherwise, you can't use the radio to give him commands."

"What's wrong with putting a gizmo in his ear?"

"A small device can fall out. And the people standing around would hear you talking."

"I still don't like it."

"We'll place it just under the skin," said Dr. Albedo. "Your cat won't feel a thing. We'll remove it as soon as possible."

"If this is unacceptable, you may leave, Miss McNabb," said Hanover. "But we'll have to scrub the mission. We have no back-up animals. We would not have asked you unless we felt confident in your ability to help us and your country. We have reports that you have trained your cat to follow your directions—not something most cats can do."

Noelle gazed into the anxious cat eyes staring back at her. She was as patriotic as any other American, but she loved her pet. "If you promise you won't hurt Ceebee. You won't give him a lobotomy or anything."

"We will treat your cat as gently as we treat our agents," said Hanover.

Destiny stifled a laugh.

"All right then." Noelle set her cat on the island. "But be careful."

"I'll leave you in the doctor's capable hands." Hanover turned to Destiny. "Let me know if any problems arise."

"Yes, sir," she replied.

Noelle was indignant. "Ceebee will do his job just fine!"

Hanover gave a 'we'll-see-about-that' look before leaving the room.

Ceebee sniffed the chemical-laden air and prowled around the island top, his ears and head lowered. His tail shot straight out with the tip moving from side to side. Noelle tried to give him some comforting pats, but Ceebee turned from her, as if say, "Why did you bring me to this awful place?" Destiny perched atop a stool, crossed her arms, and watched.

"First, we fit the collar on him." The scientist took a plastic box off a shelf, placed it on the island, opened the lid, and removed a metal ring.

"That looks awfully large," said Noelle. "Will Ceebee be able to walk in that thing?"

"We've miniaturized the electronics as much as possible," said Dr. Albedo. "Hold the cat still, please."

Noelle grabbed Ceebee around his middle. Dr. Albedo first slipped off the elastic collar from around the cat's head. He opened a segment of the metal ring, slid the device around Ceebee's neck, and fastened it. The collar was indeed big and nearly touched the ground. Ceebee shook his head and clawed at the collar with a hind paw.

Noelle tried to slip a finger between the ring and the cat's neck. "It looks tight."

"We can make some adjustments," said the scientist. "We didn't know what size animal we'd be working with."

He used a screwdriver to fine-tune the collar. Ceebee eyed him. Noelle stroked the cat to keep him calm.

"Put the animal on the floor, please," he said.

Noelle obliged. Ceebee roamed the floor, sniffing the items on the lower shelves and looking for an escape nook. The feline rubbed the collar against the wall in an effort to remove it. Dr. Albedo flipped some switches on a console panel. "Now to try the audio. Test, test, testing." His voice echoed from a wall speaker as the sound was transmitted over the microphone in the cat's collar.

"Hey, it works!" Noelle's voice came over the loudspeaker as well.

"Of course, it works," said Destiny. "Nobody at SIAMESE comes here to fail."

"We're ready to insert the earpiece," said Dr. Albedo. "You'll need to leave the animal with us overnight for the procedure. He'll be ready first thing in the morning." He picked up the cat. Ceebee squirmed, but didn't fight back. "He's a beautiful animal. I think he'll work out just fine."

Noelle gave her pet a good-bye kiss on the top of his head. "Good night, Ceebee. You be a good kitty for the man. I'll be back for you soon."

To Destiny she said, "Will someone pick me up in the morning and bring me back here?"

Destiny glanced at her wristwatch. "It's almost morning already. Why don't you crash here? Save a trip to your pad and back. We've got sleeping quarters for agents who need to grab some shuteye."

"I don't want to put you out—"

"Don't be silly. SIAMESE is like Vegas; people work here day and night."

"Now scoot along, girls," said Dr. Albedo. "We need to get started."

Noelle gave Ceebee a pat on the head and followed Destiny into the hall. They rode the elevator up a few levels to another floor. Did all the corridors in headquarters look the same? Noelle marveled that Destiny could keep track of where they were in the seemingly unending halls. Soon they arrived at a room filled with cots, chairs and lockers.

"Looks like you'll be sleeping solo," said Destiny. "Don't worry about any guys dropping by; the men's dormitory is across the hall." She opened one particular locker. "You can use my nightgown." The spy pointed to a cabinet on the opposite wall. "Soap, toothbrushes, towels are in there. Bathroom is through that door."

"You cats think of everything," said Noelle. "But won't you need your nightie?"

"I have to take care of some things."

"When do you sleep?"

"We SIAMESE cats like our catnaps. I'll pick you up for breakfast. And stay put. If you wander down the hall, you'll get lost and give the security guards a heart attack." She tapped the security badge hanging around Noelle's neck. "And don't take that off, even when you're snoozing. If someone comes in and doesn't see a badge, she'll assume you don't belong here."

"What if I need something?"

Destiny pointed to an intercom on the wall. "Push the button and give a shout. Someone will help you."

"Thanks a lot, Destiny. By the way, I was wondering . . ."

"Yes?"

Noelle sat down on one of the cots. "When we were in the briefing room and you petted Ceebee, you looked like you were a cat person."

A cloud came over Destiny's eyes. "I had a kitten once, when I was a kid growing up in the Chicago projects. Little black kitty just like yours. He lived on the street, but always came running to me when I got off the school bus. I used some of my lunch money to buy tuna for him. I sneaked him into the apartment and played with him when my mama wasn't looking. My home life wasn't so hot. The kitten was about the only thing that made the neighborhood tolerable. Then one day some stinking gang bangers got hopped-up on dope, came gunning down the street in a hot rod and ran over my kitty. Only pet I ever had."

"Destiny, that's terrible. Why don't you get another cat?"

"With my crazy hours? I'd never be home to mess with it."

"If you ever need a cat fix, you can always come over to my place and play with Ceebee. Any time."

"We'll see." Destiny shot her a smile that quickly disappeared. "Good night and sweet dreams." She hurried out of the room.

Noelle noticed that Destiny always shut down whenever they began to talk about personal matters. Or maybe Destiny became a spy so she wouldn't have to face her feelings. At any rate, Noelle was exhausted. She changed into the nightgown—a little long and roomy, but adequate. She headed in the bathroom to prepare for bed. Sweet dreams, indeed. She'd probably have nightmares about a car running over Ceebee during the mission. How could she sleep with so many questions running through her mind? What if the bad guys caught Ceebee spying on them? The enormous collar was impossible to miss. What if the collar stopped transmitting? What if Ceebee didn't cooperate? What if the police spotted them? What if—? Her bedtime prayers didn't calm her down as much as she'd hoped.

Chapter 6: Listen, People
Wednesday

The food in the SIAMESE commissary was as bland as the room itself, with its stark white walls, glaring overhead fluorescent lighting, cold gray metal tables and chairs, and no windows. The handful of agents scattered among the tables wore dark suits or dresses. Noelle and Destiny picked up their food in the cafeteria line and took their trays to a small square table. Noelle selected a hearty meal of pancakes, eggs, sausage, a sliced banana and orange juice. Destiny had lighter fare, a bowl of yogurt, fruit, berries and granola, along with a cup of coffee. She had changed into a black, long-sleeved turtleneck shirt and bell-bottoms. Noelle was back in her clothes from the day before. She felt itchy and in need of clean threads.

"Did you sleep well?" Destiny asked.

"Pretty well," said Noelle. "Took me a while to drop off."

"I thought you'd doze off right away. I left you about one a.m."

"What time is it now? I didn't wind my wristwatch, and I don't see any clocks around here." Noelle hadn't seen a single timepiece anywhere in the building.

"The clock thing is deliberate," said Destiny. "If people see the time, they feel tired and stop working."

"I have to open the record shop at ten."

"Don't worry about that. Hanover contacted your employer and got you off the hook. We need you all morning for surveillance."

"What excuse did he give my boss this time?"

"That you'd nabbed a modeling gig."

Noelle chuckled. "With my looks, nobody will believe that."

"Hurry up and eat. The doc is waiting for us."

They ate, and then picked up Ceebee from the lab. The cat was groggy from the anesthesia, so Noelle packed him into the carrier with no problem. Hanover met them in the underground parking area for a briefing. Destiny was to drive a SIAMESE van disguised as a telephone repair truck. Hanover ordered Noelle to ride in the enclosed back of the van so she wouldn't see the location of SIAMESE headquarters on their way out. Noelle argued that if he confided in her enough to risk the life of her pet, why couldn't he trust her with secrets? But he insisted that she follow orders or stay behind. So reluctantly, she sat in the back, surrounded by banks of electronic equipment. As the van left the facility, Noelle opened the crate and inspected Ceebee as he slept. He had a scar behind his right ear, the site of the earpiece implant. The surrounding skin had been shaved for the operation, so Ceebee looked like a stray tom that had lost some hair in a street fight.

They stopped at Noelle's house long enough for Ceebee, now awake, to use the litter box and eat a bowl of kibble. Noelle picked up some cat treats and changed into a plaid shirt, blue jeans, socks and sneakers. Over their clothes, the women slipped on gray overalls with a phone company patch on the left breast. They were off, this time with Noelle riding shotgun in the cab with Ceebee on her lap. As long as she held the cat, he was happy, and she didn't need the carrier.

As they drove down the highway to Riverbend, Noelle asked, "What do you know about SPARK?"

Destiny was confused. "Spark?"

"Spiritually Pure And Radiant Kin. It's a cult run by a guy who calls himself the Wise One."

"I don't keep up on the news unless it affects a mission."

"There's a bunch of SPARK devotees in Yuletide. I think something weird is going on."

"Weird how?"

"I can't tell if the kids in the group are brainwashed or not. On the surface they seem happy, but I think something odd is going on behind the smiles and singing. One of them is scared, but she wouldn't tell me why."

"That doesn't interest us. SIAMESE can't go after every con artist."

"Oh, well. Can I listen to the radio? I need some music to wake me up."

Destiny switched on the car radio and scanned through the local stations. Noelle asked her to stop tuning when they heard an advertisement about SPARK. A D.J. stated that the Wise One would be holding a public teaching rally tomorrow afternoon at the large park near the zoo in west Riverbend. Free admission, all invited. A group of devotees sang a bright jingle to close out the ad.

"Sounds like SPARK is looking for more recruits," said Noelle.

"Interesting," Destiny mused. "And you and I were just talking about them. Dash says there are no coincidences."

Destiny took the highway exit ramp and switched off the radio. After a couple of miles, she pulled into downtown Riverbend, the old part of town, and soon reached a public park carved out of a grassy area along the Ohio River. The tiny park attracted few tourists and was used mainly by those living in the nearby low-cost apartment buildings—as well as drug dealers and other ne'er-do-wells. The park offered few amenities, just a slide and two swings as a playground, and a couple of wooden benches that were marked with graffiti and facing the water. A clump of straggly trees surrounded the park. Destiny parked along the curb beside a line of telephone poles. The women and the cat retreated into the enclosed back of the van. The women sat in metal chairs that faced a console; Ceebee lay on the floor with paws tucked under and tail twitching. Destiny turned on a device that raised a telescopic pole atop the van. A video camera topped the pole. Destiny used a joystick on the console to maneuver the camera until they had a clear view of the park on a black-and-white monitor.

The spy said, "The info we intercepted said the meeting would take place here."

"How do we know which one is Old Scratch?"

"Process of elimination. Won't be too many men in a park on a weekday."

"What if Old Scratch is a woman?"

Destiny shot her partner a look. "You watch too much TV."

Several pedestrians wandered in and out of view of the camera: mothers pushing strollers and a couple of joggers in sweatsuits, hugging and puffing along. Eventually a lone man appeared. In the cool weather, he didn't seem out of place wearing a long coat. Even with a felt-brimmed hat pulled over his face, one could see he was a black man. He sat on a bench and opened a newspaper.

"That's the contact." Destiny flipped the "record" switch on the van's videotape machine that was connected to the camera.

"How can you tell?"

"He isn't reading. His eyes are on the people, not the paper."

Indeed, after several minutes the man still hadn't turned a page.

Destiny worked the zoom lens to enlarge the man's features. "He doesn't look familiar to me. The boys back at HQ will look over the tape to see if he matches anyone in our files."

A second man arrived. He was bundled up in a coat, gloves, a stocking cap and dark glasses. A scarf was wound around his nose and mouth. He sat on the far side of the bench, acting as if he didn't notice the other man.

Destiny swore. "Old Scratch is wrapped up like a mummy. We can't see his face."

"Can you park the van closer and zoom in?" said Noelle.

"No, this is as close as we can get without looking obvious. Okay, this is it." Destiny pushed an activation button on Ceebee's collar. "Let the cat out."

Noelle's heart pounded as she grabbed the pet, opened the rear door, and jumped from the van. She couldn't mess up now. She pointed Ceebee in the direction of the men.

"Ceebee, see that bench? Go there. You have to go to the bench." She set the cat on the ground and gave Ceebee a treat. Then she tossed a second treat in the direction of the bench. "Go!"

Over the years she'd train Ceebee with the hope of taking him to Hollywood and putting him in movies. One of the tricks he'd learn was to go in a specific direction. Now Noelle held her breath to see if Ceebee would follow orders. The cat ran to the goodie and wolfed it down. He looked back at his master for another treat. She pointed to the bench, and then got back in the van. She shut the door and resumed her seat beside Density in front of the TV monitor. Ceebee began walking toward the woods. As the cat walked, the sensitive collar mic picked up a soft breeze along with the rustle of the grass and the faint sounds of children playing on the swings.

"How do I talk to Ceebee?" Noelle asked.

"Use that." Destiny pointed to a microphone on the console.

Noelle leaned into the mic. "Ceebee, go to the bench. The bench!" The cat looked around and ambled toward the target. "See! He's doing it!"

"Hold your hat on, sister. We're not there yet. There's another twenty feet to go."

Somebody pounded on the van door. The women exchanged anxious glances.

"The cops?" asked Noelle. "Are we parked illegally?"

Destiny whispered, "Keep your voice down." She rose, opened the door a crack, and peered out. "Yes?"

An elderly woman in a housecoat, moccasins and a windbreaker stood beside the van. "Are you here to fix our reception?"

"What?"

"I live over there." The woman pointed to an apartment building across the street. "We've been getting a lot of static on our phone line. Can you please come and fix it?"

"Maybe later. We have to work on these lines first before we do anything else."

"That's a funny looking cherry picker you got."

"Cherry picker?"

"That thing on top of your van."

"Oh, that." Destiny frowned. "It's a new gizmo we're trying out so we can look at the phone wires without climbing the pole. Now if you'll excuse me, I have to get back to work."

"Thanks. Don't forget, apartment 312. I'll be waiting for you."

Density nodded and shut the door. She resumed her seat and sighed. "I gotta tell Dash we need a better disguise for our vans."

Outside, Ceebee slowly continued his trek toward the bench. A mother with a boy in tow came into view of the camera.

The collar mic picked up the kid's voice. "Look at the kitty! I wanna pet the kitty!"

Noelle glanced at her partner in alarm. What if the kid sees the collar?

She spoke into the mic. "Ceebee, move away. Go."

But the cat stopped, eyed the boy and swished his tail.

The boy took two steps toward the cat, with his arms outstretched. "Here, kitty, kitty. I wanna play with kitty!"

But the mother grabbed the boy's hand and pulled him back. "Leave that creature alone! It's covered in fleas."

Noelle exclaimed, "Ceebee does not have fleas!"

Destiny slapped her hand over the microphone. "Quiet!"

Noelle covered her mouth. "Sorry."

The mom dragged the boy away. Ceebee started to follow them.

"No, Ceebee, no," Noelle spoke softly into the mic. "The bench. Go to the bench."

With a flick of her hand, Destiny swiveled the outside camera to follow the cat. Ceebee trundled along, slowed by the heavy collar. He stopped to sniff the grass or an insect.

"Can't you hurry your feline?" said Destiny. "We need to hear what the guys are saying before they leave."

"Okay, okay. Cats can be finicky." Noelle spoke into the mic. "Ceebee, go. Go now. Go to the bench." Ceebee finally reached his destination.

"Stay, Ceebee. Stay." And just like a dog, the cat lay down near the feet of Old Scratch "Good boy. Stay." The cat put his head on his paws.

"Is the cat sleeping?" Destiny asked.

"If he is, he won't move."

Destiny switched on a reel-to-reel tape machine to capture the conversation, as the TV camera only recorded visual, not audio. The man with the newspaper folded the pages and laid them on his lap. He gazed at the trees and spoke without looking at the other man. The men's voices came over the speaker, a bit faint but audible.

The newspaper reader spoke first. "Nice time of day for plowing the fields."

The man in the stocking cap and scarf took a small metal cylinder from his coat pocket. He pressed the tip of the gadget against his voice box. "The farmers are expecting a bumper crop of wheat." His voice was monotone and distorted, like a computer speaking.

"What's he doing?" Noelle asked.

"It's a voice scrambler," Destiny explained. "Smart move on his part. Keeps the other guy from recognizing his voice. But it doesn't help us get an I.D. on him."

The first man continued. "Heavy rain is predicted for the weekend."

"But the sun will still shine in Kentucky," said the second.

Noelle rested her elbows on the counter and put her chin on her fists. "They're just farmers talking about their crops."

"Shhhh! They're exchanging passwords."

"Oh."

The newspaper guy crossed his legs and still looked away. "What have you got to sell?"

"Preliminary specs on an American satellite."

The man shook his head. "Not good enough. We need hard data. Final blueprints. Sketches mean nothing. Hardware can be overhauled many times before the final draft."

"But it's more powerful than Sputnik."

"Our files are overflowing with satellite schematics. We need something else."

"What would you like?" asked Old Scratch.

"Weapons. Ammunition. I can only sell satellites to the big countries. Guns, I can unload anywhere."

"The local manufacturers only make rifles for hunting ducks and shooting tin cans. You'll need to look elsewhere for military-type arms."

"Perhaps I shall."

"Wait!" Old Scratch laid a hand on the other man's arm. The man with the newspaper jerked his arm away. "I have an idea."

Ceebee raised his head with a start, stared intently at the trees, and then ran.

"Ceebee! No!" Noelle yelled into the mic. "Stay! Stay!"

"Why is he running?" asked Destiny.

"I don't know. Ceebee! Come back!"

Destiny swung the camera around to follow the errant cat. Ceebee darted into the trees and out of camera range. Noelle kept calling for the pet to return to no avail.

Destiny slumped back in her seat. "That rips it. I thought you had the animal trained."

"I do. I—listen." Noelle held up a hand.

Over the speaker came the sound of the cat running, then some squeaks and a bit of a rustling in the grass. The noises stopped for a moment, and then they heard teeth chomping something crunchy.

"Oh dear," said Noelle. "Ceebee caught a mouse. I guess technology is no match for Mother Nature."

"Is the critter going to stay in the woods all day, feeding his face?"

"He has a name. I thought you liked cats."

"Not when they scoot off during a mission."

"Ceebee will be back. He always comes home after he goes hunting."

Destiny moved the camera back on the men. They could see the spies, but not hear them. Old Scratch stood and walked away.

"The target is moving," said Density.

"Are we going to follow him?"

"We'd look too suspicious in these clothes. Anyway, we need to retrieve the collar. That's a pricey piece of hardware."

"What about retrieving the cat attached to the collar?" said Noelle.

"Yeah, that too."

Noelle sprang up and opened the back door. Before Destiny could object, she leapt out of the van and hurried into the trees. The park bench was empty—both men had left, going in separate directions, so neither one saw Noelle.

"Ceebee! Ceebee!" she called.

The cat shuffled out from the trees. He licked his chops, content.

"Come here, you silly mouser." Noelle picked up the cat. "A fine time for you to go hunting."

When Noelle returned to the van, a peeved Destiny was waiting outside the cab. She pulled open the passenger door and spoke crossly. "Get in."

Soon they were back on the road. Noelle petted the cat seated on her lap. "What now?"

"You and the animal are going home. I need to file my report with Hanover. He won't be happy."

"It wasn't a total loss. We know the collar works. We know Old Scratch is selling weapons."

"But we don't know if he's working for himself or a boss. Or what he plans on selling or when." Destiny took the on-ramp to the freeway heading for Yuletide. "But we know one thing."

"What's that?"

"His contact wasn't a Russian. One, the Reds don't use blacks in their operations. Two, the Ruskies buy weapons for their own stockpile, not to pass onto somebody else. Remember in our last mission, I said we had a wild card? We got a third party muscling in on the Cold War. Things are going to get a lot chillier as they heat up."

"Is the guy who's buying an American?"

"I think so. Had a Southern tang to his voice."

"Why isn't Old Scratch selling his secrets to the Russians?"

"Maybe he is. The more buyers, the merrier. The dirty traitor can up the price with a bidding war."

"Can I take the collar off Ceebee?"

"No. Hanover might want to use acoustic cat again, preferably some place without rodents."

Chapter 7: Out And About

After Destiny pulled up in front of Noelle's house, the actress lit from the cab and dropped Ceebee on the ground so he could play outside. But with the heavy collar, the cat didn't feel energetic, so Ceebee found a spot in the sun and slept, worn out by his spy work. Noelle stripped off her SIAMESE-issued overalls and handed them back to Destiny. As the spy drove off, Noelle toyed with the idea of following her in the Bug to find the location of SIAMESE headquarters. But a sharp agent like Destiny would know she was being tailed and would lead her on a wild goose chase.

Noelle went inside the house and called her mom to get the scoop on the town meeting the night before. She was dying to find out what the city had planned to do with the hippie visitors. The phone rang at the McNabb house, but nobody answered. Mom was probably out shopping or attending one of her daytime women's clubs. Noelle phoned the *Herald* office. As she suspected, Trevor had attended the gathering.

"Hi, Noelle. I'm writing up the story as we speak." Over the phone Noelle heard the quick, precise clacking of an electric typewriter. Trevor wedged the phone receiver between his ear and shoulder as he typed. "It was quite a hoo-haw."

"Can I get a sneak peek at what you're writing?"

"Say, where were you last night? You like to keep up on the local dirt."

"I had to babysit the twins."

"Tell you what, Noelle. I'm heading out to the campgrounds to get some quotes for my story. None of the sparklettes showed up at the lynching last night. If you can meet me at the *Herald* office toot sweet, you can ride along and I'll fill you in."

Noelle quickly changed into a casual blue dress with buttons down the front, a notch-lapel collar and sash belt. Pantyhose, flats, silver earrings and a light coat completed the ensemble. She zipped into town in the Bug and parked in the lot behind the *Herald* building. Soon she was riding along in Trevor's coupe, on their way to the devotees' lair. Trevor was dressed in brown corduroy pants and matching jacket along with a red turtleneck sweater.

As usual, Trevor drove too fast, as he was always in a hurry. "The meeting got pretty heated last night. A lot of ugly things were said."

"That's a shame," said Noelle. "People in Yuletide are a bit old-fashioned, but I never thought they were nasty."

"They're just ignorant. Anything unfamiliar is peculiar. The local folk think the world ends at the city limits."

They stopped at a red light. "Did they run the devotees out of town?" she asked.

"They can't do that. The only charges they have on the cult are disturbing the peace and public annoyance, nothing worse than what the Saturday night drunks do. So, the town council passed a bunch of resolutions that won't pass muster legally but made everyone feel better. The sparkles can't hang around the schools or beg for money on the streets or hand out brochures."

The light changed, and Trevor sped on. "Then the citizens found out that First Sage had filed for a permit to use Poinsettia Park for a rally this weekend. The townsfolk wanted to put the bosh on that, but our good mayor said that as long as the group had paid for a permit—which they did—and don't sell alcohol in the park—which they won't—they could hold their shindig."

"Do you think there's going to be trouble at the rally?"

Trevor chuckled. "I don't think so. I can't picture our illustrious police chief dealing with a jail full of hippies."

The reporter parked his coupe in the lot just inside the entrance to Holiday Acres. Trevor and Noelle took the well-worn dirt path going north and up the side of a large hill to a grassy lawn. The young people were standing in a circle, moving clockwise as they sang, danced and banged on tambourines.

First Sage intercepted the intruders. He had fire in his eyes. "What do you want?"

"I'm Trevor Spellman, reporter for the *Yuletide Herald*."

"Haven't your people done enough to us already?"

"I'm here to get your side of the story. Why were you or a representative of SPARK absent from the town meeting last night?"

First Sage glanced at the pen and notebook in Trevor's hands. He took a deep breath to compose himself. He straightened his back and his calm demeanor returned. "The devotees knew they would not be welcome. We have no wish to incite trouble or displease our hosts."

"What is your reaction to the resolution passed by the council?"

"We are disappointed, of course. We are sorry if we offended anyone in our zeal to share the good news of our message. We are so enthusiastic about our convictions, that pagans—I mean, that others often misinterpret our actions."

Noelle thought his speech sounded memorized, as if First Sage had recited the piece repeatedly in other towns.

Trevor asked, "Do you plan to remain in Yuletide or will you be moving on after your rally?"

"We live under the guidance of the Wise One. He is the one who selects our mission fields and when we come and go."

"When do I get to speak with this Wise One?"

Noelle interrupted. "Where's Blossom?"

First Sage shifted his gaze to her. "Pardon me?"

"I don't see Blossom dancing with the others."

He cast his eye on the circle. "She may be in a guidance talk with one of our coaches. They are older devotees who have been with us a long time and are more spiritually advanced. They counsel our novices who need a helping hand. Blossom is a sweet girl, but she requires a little more attention than most of our children."

A glint came to Trevor's eye. "Is there any truth to a report that Blossom was frightened by someone associated with SPARK?"

A look of confusion, and then anger, crossed First Sage's face. "Where did you hear such a ridiculous rumor? Of course not. Each and every child of SPARK is treated with love and respect at all times."

Noelle slipped her handbag inside her coat so the men wouldn't see it. "I left my purse in the car. Would you excuse me, please?"

She headed partway down the hill toward the parking lot. But when she was out of sight of First Sage, she ducked behind the trees and doubled back to the cabins in hopes of finding Blossom on her own. Perhaps the girl was in the ladies' room. Perhaps she was sick and resting in her cabin. Or perhaps whatever Blossom feared had come to pass. Noelle wasn't convinced by First Sage's explanation. For someone who seemed to be on top of things, how could he overlook a missing devotee?

Upon reaching the Shawnee cabin, Noelle peered into the back window. The building was empty. Blossom was not on her bunk, but a white, letter-size envelope and a sheet of paper were laid on the blanket. Noelle slipped into the cabin and picked up the folded notepaper. A message in black ink had been hand-written in all capitals.

"URGENT. MUST SPEAK TO YOU IMMEDIATELY. MEET ME AT FIRE PIT."

A cold dread came over Noelle. Blossom must have read this note and gone to the fire pit, the place where groups held their campfires and cooked hot dogs and s'mores. But how did the letter get to her? The envelope had no address or stamp. The letter had no signature or name. Someone must have sneaked into the campgrounds and either hand delivered the message to Blossom or left it in the cabin.

Or maybe someone already present in the camp had left the note.

Noelle folded the paper, placed it in the envelope and tucked it into her purse. She left the cabin and followed a gravel path through the woods and down the hill. She trod carefully, lest a tree branch snag her hose. Thank goodness she had the foresight to wear flats and not heels for walking the rugged trail. Finally, the trees cleared and she trod slowly downhill to keep her balance.

At the bottom of the hill stood a large lake, ringed with a wide, muddy shoreline. A squirrel ran into the forest that grew a few yards beyond the shore. The birds chipped nosily as Noelle picked her way among the twigs and dead leaves that carpeted the shore. Some faint footprints were visible, but impossible to identify. The prints could belong Mr. Woodman, a security guard or any of the devotees who had come this way for a private meditation. The site was bursting with nature's glory, and had been a favorite place for Noelle to come and relax during summer camps. The sun glinted off the still waters of the lake. Noelle followed the shore to a clearing that held the stone fire pit. Rows of wooden benches were set in a semicircle that faced the lake and the pit.

Noelle found the body half-hidden beneath one of the benches.

Chapter 8: As Tears Go By

Noelle ran up the hill, her feet slipping in the gravel. Soon she reached the cabins. The devotees were seated in a circle on the lawn. They listened raptly to First Sage, who stood in the center of the gathering. He was giving a lecture on mental purity, reading from notes attached to a brown wooden clipboard held in his hand. Trevor was standing outside the circle, scribbling in his notebook. Noelle stopped a few yards away and frantically gestured for Trevor to come to her. The reporter gave her a questioning look. She waved again.

Trevor joined Noelle. "Where have you been?"

She panted, still winded from her dash up the hill. "I found Blossom!"

"And?" He didn't sound concerned.

"She's dead."

"What! Dead? Are you sure?"

She glanced at the devotees. "Keep your voice down!" Noelle was gasping in between words. "I saw her—her body—at the fire pit—by the lake."

Trevor looked off at the trees, as if gathering his thoughts. "All right. You tell First Sage. I'll go to the office and call the police. I'll have the *Herald* send over a photographer."

"Trevor! Can't you ever stop being a nosy reporter for once?"

"No. Never. This is hot news. Now scram." Before she could object, Trevor raced down the dirt path to the building near the front gate that housed the camp office.

Noelle was fearful of First Sage's reaction to her news. Would he accuse her of foul play? Was he somehow responsible for the tragedy? True, he'd been near the cabins since she and Trevor had arrived, but Blossom's death may have occurred hours ago.

First Sage was leading the group in a chant. Noelle approached the circle. She didn't want to upset the devotees, who looked so peaceful and happy. Noelle stepped around the seated youths and walked up to First Sage. She whispered in his ear. "I need to speak to you."

"Will you please leave us alone?" He was irritated, but spoke softly so the devotees would not hear. "We are busy with our group devotion."

"I found Blossom."

"Tell her to come and join us."

"She—she can't move."

"Is she sick? Did she break her leg?" He sounded concerned.

"Can we please move outside the circle? I don't want to bother the others."

A look of annoyance flashed over his eyes, but First Sage followed Noelle a short distance away from the followers. "Please be brief," he said. "I have no time for guessing games."

Noelle said as calmly as she could, "Blossom is dead."

A dark cloud covered First Sage's face. His voice was low, but angry. "Take your stupid joke and get out of here!"

"It's true, it's true! She's on the ground by the lake."

"For heaven's sake. Blossom must have wandered away and fallen asleep."

"People don't crawl under benches and sleep on the ground. Her limbs are twisted. Her face is pale. She looks terrible."

"Where is the girl? I'll put a stop to this foolishness."

"This way."

Noelle started along the gravel path that went down the hill. She heard the sound of sandals slapping on the ground behind her, so she knew First Sage was following. Neither of them said a word as they hurried.

If First Sage was the killer, he and Blossom could have easily slipped away from the group earlier in the day with no one noticing. The devotees are too engrossed in their activities to notice the world around them. If First Sage decided to get rid of Noelle as well, he could toss her body into the lake or bury it in the woods. Trevor would never find a hidden body. Then again, if First Sage had killed Blossom, he would avoid suspicion by hiding the body and claiming that she had run away. Too many questions and no way to get the answers.

Noelle and First Sage approached the fire pit. When he saw the body, he gasped and put his hands to his mouth. First Sage knelt beside the corpse and gently touched Blossom's face. He felt for a pulse in the wrist and neck.

First Sage looked at Noelle. Tears welled up in his eyes. "Is this how you found her?"

"Yes. I haven't touched a thing."

He nodded, stood up, and said nothing for a moment. He took a deep breath. "This is very sad. She was one of our most delightful girls."

Noelle said, "Trevor is calling the police. They should be here soon."

"You go and meet them. I will wait here." He sank onto one of the benches.

"Just a minute. How do I know you won't move the body while I'm gone?"

First Sage glared at her. "Do you honestly believe I did this?"

"Well, no, I—" She let the sentence trail off.

He stared out at the water. "You pagans treat us like dirt."

She sat on a bench on the opposite side of the fire pit. "I'll wait with you."

First Sage pressed his palms together, rested his fingertips on his forehead and bowed his head. He rocked steadily back and forth as he emitted a low, dirge-like chant, as if he were saying a prayer for the dead. Noelle made her own silent prayer as well, for the sake of Blossom's soul and for wisdom on how to handle the situation. Together they kept an uncomfortable vigil.

After what seemed like ages, the tramping of feet and loud voices from the path interrupted their thoughts. Trevor led the procession down the hill to the shore, followed by Chief Whitlock; Dr. Robert, the chief administrator at the local St. Nicolas Hospital and the closest thing the town had to a coroner; two paramedics carrying a gurney; a photographer from the *Herald*; Mr. Woodman; and several devotees.

Whitlock spotted First Sage sitting on the bench. He snorted. "You again!"

First Sage removed his glasses and wiped them off with the sleeve of his robe. He set the frames back on his face and stood up, seemingly composed and in charge again. He approached his people. "Go back, children. You do not need to see this."

"Trying to hide something?" Whitlock asked.

"No, of course not. My only wish is that the children are not distressed or alarmed."

Chakra said, "Forgive us, First Sage, but we heard something happened to Blossom. We want to help if we can."

"The evil forces have attacked us," said First Sage. "I beg you, children, return to your cabins. This will only cloud your minds and distract you from the light of goodness."

"Nobody leaves until we figure out what's going on," said the chief.

The doctor squatted beside the body, trying not to dirty his suit. He quickly looked over the corpse. "I'd say death was caused by illegal drugs."

"How can you be so sure?" Noelle asked.

"Simple." Dr. Robert lifted Blossom's right hand to reveal an empty hypodermic needle on the ground.

"Don't touch that," said Whitlock. "Fingerprints."

"Hey, now, that's not the real deal. No way, man," said Chakra. "She was clean. Blossom never did no junk. She wasn't a druggie."

"He's right," said First Sage. "Among the devotees we have a strict rule forbidding all intoxicating substances."

"There's the needle," said the doctor, "and here are the marks." He raised the corpse's left arm. The sleeve of the robe fell back, revealing fresh needle holes.

The devotees cried.

"That settles it," said Whitlock. "A hippie dies of an overdose. Happens all the time."

"Shouldn't you do an autopsy before you jump to conclusions?" Noelle asked.

Whitlock glared at her. "What else could it be? The girl didn't croak from old age."

The doctor turned to the cameraman. "Can you take some pictures before we move the body?"

"No, no, you mustn't print such things in the newspaper!" First Sage sounded worried.

"It's all right," said Trevor. "We're a community newspaper, not a tabloid. The pictures are strictly for police use." He glanced at Whitlock. "Isn't that right, chief?"

"Hmm? Oh, yeah, sure." Whitlock scratched his head. "Hurry up and let's get this over with."

As the photographer snapped away, the devotees began to wail. First Sage put his arms around his people and comforted them. "Now, children, remember that Blossom's spirit is among the universe now, free and pure. Do not stay in sorrow. Return to that special place of joy within your hearts. Death is just a passing from one plane of existence into another."

Noelle watched the photog at work. Something bothered her about the body, but she couldn't place it. When the cameraman finished his work, he stepped back so the medics could pull out the body from beneath the bench and load it onto the gurney. As they did, the corpse's left arm dropped and dangled over the side of the stretcher.

"Wait!" Noelle shouted. "Something's wrong."

"Now what?" Whitlock grumbled.

"Blossom was left-handed. On Monday, when I was in the park and handed her the beach ball, she took it with her left hand." She looked at the devotees. "Is that correct? Was Blossom a southpaw?"

They murmured among themselves. "Yeah, I think so," said a girl. "Whenever Wise One taught us, she took notes with her left hand."

"Then the needle marks should be in her right arm," said Noelle. "A drug user would most likely shoot up with the dominant hand."

"Maybe she was ambidextrous," said Whitlock. "Or she'd already ruined all the veins in her right arm."

"I don't think so," she replied. "Doctor, can we please see her right arm?" Dr. Robert lifted the limb. "See, no needle scars at all."

Whitlock pursed his lips. "How come you know so much about using drugs?"

Noelle frowned at him. "I read about these things in books."

Trevor said, "So maybe someone else made the injection?"

"But we all loved Blossom," said Chakra. "Nobody wanted to hurt her. She was a sweet little lamb. Who would do such a horrible thing?"

Mr. Woodman assured the group that the security guard had reported nothing suspicious from the night before and had seen no trespassers.

"This is a pretty big camp," said Trevor. "It'd be easy for an intruder to slip in. One security guard can't be everywhere."

Whitlock cleared his throat. "I think y'all making this a lot more complicated that it is. The girl died of a drug overdose."

"We know that," said Noelle, "but was it self-inflicted or murder?"

The devotees were still crying. First Sage tugged at Whitlock's jacket sleeve. "Please, I must see to the children's welfare. Do what you have to do here, but we must leave this evil place. I will speak to you later about recovering the body. We must give the girl the final ritual so that her soul will be at rest."

"I think it's best if you all just packed up and moved out of town," said Whitlock.

"Leave?" First Sage was indignant. "How can we go when we have so many questions about our daughter?" He gestured at the body.

The chief threw back his shoulders and hiked up his belt. "You folks have been nothin' but trouble since you arrived. We don't need any more of your—"

First Sage raised his voice. "You cannot blame this death upon us! We do not kill our children!" The devotees stared, incredulous, at their leader. He softened his tone. "Forgive me, my children. I am not allowing my inner peace to rule my words."

Mr. Woodman jumped into the conversation. "Chief Whitlock, these folks are paid up through next Monday. They've kept the grounds clean and neat, and they've been polite and quiet, which is more than I can say for some of the folks who camp here. As far as I'm concerned, they can stay. I'd rather not refund their money if I don't have to."

Whitlock eyed the camp director. "If you don't mind, this is official police business!"

"In that case," said Noelle, "you should let the devotees remain in town until the investigation's over."

The chief turned on her. "Are you telling me how to do my job, missy?"

Noelle smirked but said nothing.

First Sage turned to the reporter. "Can we please keep this incident out of the newspapers?"

"I agree with him," Mr. Woodman. "Might scare off our summer tourists if they hear about bad doings on the grounds."

"I'm afraid not," Trevor said. "A free press is the bedrock of a democracy. The public has a right to know."

"The public hates us," said First Sage. "When they hear of this terrible thing, they will assume the worst. They may even try to harm us. It will cause great damage to the SPARK movement."

"I'm sorry, First Sage," said Trevor. "My job is to report all the news, the good and the bad. But I promise to be fair in my story."

"Fair!" First Sage spat on the ground. "Come, children. We must leave the pagans to their ways." He turned on his heel, and tramped to the gravel path. The devotees followed him up the hill, singing a sad song of loss and pain as they walked.

The medics hoisted the gurney and left as well. The photographer departed to develop his prints in the darkroom at the *Herald* office.

"I should have the groundskeeper clean up this area," said Mr. Woodman "No blood, thankfully."

"Shouldn't we look for evidence first?" said Noelle.

Whitlock glared at her. "Are you still on this murder kick?"

"Yes, I am. I knew Blossom. She'd never use drugs. And if she did, how did she get the needle and dope? She couldn't walk into town and buy them."

"Maybe somebody mailed them to her," said Whitlock.

"All of the mail for the campers comes to my office," said Mr. Woodman, "and I distribute it to them. No packages have arrived this week for any of the guests. And rest assured we've had no drug dealers on the grounds, only the boy from the grocery store who brought in food for the campers. Now if all of you would clear out of here in the next ten minutes, I'd appreciate it. Nobody's supposed to be on the grounds anyway unless they've paid for the night. And please," he spoke directly to Whitlock, "get rid of that thing"—he pointed at the needle—"before some kid picks it up."

After the camp director left, Noelle said, "That's evidence, chief. Don't lose it."

The chief glowered at her. "You better lose that smarty pants attitude, missy."

Noelle bit her tongue to keep from making a comment that might land her in jail.

Whitlock wrapped his handkerchief around the syringe, careful not to get his own fingerprints on it, and stuck the needle in his jacket pocket. As he stalked away, he muttered to no one in particular, "These dang hippies are more trouble than they're worth."

After the chief had left, Noelle sank onto a bench, exhausted. She gazed at the spot where, only moments before, a lovely human being had breathed her last.

Trevor sat down beside her. "I'm sorry, Noelle. From what you told me, Blossom sounded like a really nice girl."

Noelle kept staring at the ground. "None of this makes sense. She didn't use drugs. I know it."

"I'd say someone else was involved."

"You're right. But who was it? Someone from outside or in the cult? Here, look at this." Noelle handed him the note she'd picked up from in the cabin. "I found this on Blossom's bunk right before I came here."

Trevor read the paper. "The letter writer was the one who brought her the drugs. Or he killed her first and then planted the needle as a cover-up."

"But who? The person in SPARK who made Blossom afraid? Another devotee? Someone in her past life?"

"My guess is it's an internal job. Does anyone outside of SPARK even know she's here?" Trevor glanced at his watch. "We better get going before Mr. Woodman kicks us out. We can talk about this on the way into town."

As they trudged the steep path up the hill, Noelle asked, "If Blossom's death was murder, do you think the other devotees may be in danger?"

"I can't imagine why, unless someone else in the group is using drugs," said Trevor.

The climb was too steep for walking and talking, so the two said nothing more until they reached the top of the hill, where they paused for a moment to catch their breath. The lawn by the cabins was empty; the devotees were inside the dining hall to mourn their loss.

"I need to talk to First Sage," said Noelle. "See what he knows about Blossom's former life outside the cult."

Trevor put his hands on her shoulders. "Whoa, there, cowgirl. Now is not the best time to speak with First Sage about anything. He's too riled up. And remember, you're not a cop. You can't make people confess."

"If Whitlock won't do his job, someone has to."

"That's my girl. Spunky and bold. But impulsive. Let's sit on this for a while instead of barging in and making fools of ourselves."

"You're a reporter. You can talk to people."
"Right now, I'm a reporter on deadline. But I wouldn't worry about First Sage. The sparklettes won't be going anywhere for a while."

"If he's guilty, won't the devotees pack up and leave tonight?"

"If they do, they won't get far. Their tour bus is pretty hard to miss."

Chapter 9: Is This What You Want?

Noelle looked at her watch. "It's almost six o'clock. Are you coming to church tonight?"

"'fraid not," said Trevor. "I need to file my story before the paper goes to press tonight. You'll have to sing extra loud on the hymns to cover for me."

They sped into town in the GTO. Trevor parked in the *Herald* lot and ran inside to write his scoop. Noelle brushed the dirt off her clothes and drove straight to Bethlehem Community Church, which members affectionately called Old Beth. She didn't have time to go home and change clothes, but the midweek program was more casual than the Sunday morning service, so the dress she had on was good enough. Noelle arrived shortly after six o'clock, right in time for the potluck dinner that preceded the program. She needed the food, as she hadn't eaten since her hearty breakfast at SIAMESE headquarters. A good-sized crowd of kids, teens and adults had already gathered in the church basement. Noelle picked up a paper plate from the beginning of the buffet line loaded with casseroles, stews, fried chicken, salads and desserts. After filling a plate, she found an empty chair beside her mother in the middle of a long folding table.

"I saved you a seat." Mom raised her voice so her daughter could hear over the hubbub of other conversations. "I was getting worried that you wouldn't show up."

"I had a busy day," said Noelle.

"What, some pop group stopped by the record store?" her father joked.

Noelle struggled to remember the cover story SIAMESE had concocted for her. "No, I was on a modeling assignment in Riverbend."

"That sounds exciting," said Mom. "Pass the salt, please. Did you model for one of those fashion stores?"

Before Noelle could respond, another couple took the seats across the table and engaged her parents in conversation, sparing Noelle the necessity of thinking up another lie. She hated keeping her spy work a secret from her parents. She used to confide in her mom about everything, but now she had to be evasive. Noelle worried how she could keep her occasional fibs from becoming a habit. She set to work on her food, but had only taken a few bites when her nemesis, Gus E. Monty, an insurance agent and amorous bachelor, slid into the vacant chair beside her. He wasn't carrying a plate, which made Noelle rightly guess he was here not to eat but to bother her.

"Well, hello, Noelle," he said sprightly.

"Hi, Gus." Her response was more subdued.

"What's cookin' with you?"

"Same old, same old."

"One of my co-workers at the insurance office has a cabin on the lake. He's invited some folks, including yours truly, up there for the weekend. Wanna come?"

Noelle inwardly groaned. Two whole days of trying to evade Gus' groping hands? No thanks. "What would we be doing at this cabin on the lake?"

"All sorts of things. Fishing."

"I don't like fishing."

Gus smiled lewdly. "Depends on what you're fishing for."

She eyed him. "You won't catch a thing with the wrong bait."

"In the evening we can tell ghost stories over a campfire."

"Followed by a panty raid. That was boring back in 4-H camp."

"I never figured you to be such a party pooper."

"Will you excuse me, please? I want to finish my dinner before the program begins."

"Oh, sure, sure. I need to snag a slice of your mom's delicious blackberry pie. She's the best pie baker in town. Catch you later, alligator."

To her relief, he departed for the dessert table. But her respite was short lived when Julia slid into the folding chair that Gus had just vacated. The girls briefly exchanged hellos before Julia got to the point.

"What I wanted to ask you, Noelle, was if you could be one of the bridesmaids for my wedding?"

Noelle stopped chewing her food. The question startled her. It took a minute to shift her mindset from Blossom's death to happy nuptials. "Oh! I thought you had your wedding party set."

"Well, I did, but Jill had to back out. Some sort of summer college internship came through at the last minute. It's in Ohio, and she isn't sure she can make it back to town for my wedding. And you always seem to be hanging around town. So, can you do it?"

Noelle frowned. "I'm your number two fill-in?"

"If you'd rather not—"

"I'd be delighted to do it."

Noelle really wanted to say "no." She was miffed at Julia for taking her for granted, and anyway, she thought the whole bridesmaid bit was silly—doing nothing but standing stiffly on high heels during a dull ceremony, and spending money on an ugly dress she'd never wear again. But, as much as Noelle hated to admit it, she was jealous of the other girls who were popular enough to win a spot in every local bridal party.

"Thanks! Now I won't have to cancel my order for the fourth bridesmaid bouquet and gift."

Julia started jabbering about the wedding, which would be held in Old Beth church, of course, but Noelle only half listened.

"Hate to cut you off, Julia, but I don't have a pencil to write things down." Actually, Noelle always carried a pen and notebook in her purse, but with Blossom's death she wasn't in the mood to deal with gowns and rehearsal dinners. "Can you call me later when I'm at home and give me the dates and the details?"

"Oh, sure, sure. Anyway, I need to get back to my fiancée. He got a night off from work, so he's here tonight." Julia took off for another table.

Being a bridesmaid—just what Noelle needed, one more thing to juggle around her jobs, spy work and sleuthing. But Julia's wedding wasn't until summer, so she pushed it to the back of her mind. Noelle had gulped down most of her meal before the Christian education director of Old Beth opened the evening program with a prayer, and the youth guitar band led the members in singing up-tempo arrangements of "Holy, Holy, Holy" and "Come Thou Font of Every Blessing."

Then everyone departed to their respective classrooms by age groups: the kids to their crafts and Bible stories, the youth to a rap session, and the adults to either choir practice or a discussion group. Noelle made her way to a basement room for the Modern Social Issues class. Maybe an evening of talk about mundane community problems would take her mind off Blossom's death. The other adults, with their cups of coffee, settled in the circle of folding chairs.

Sam, the group moderator and the only person in the room wearing a suit and tie, began talking about modern-day cults. Much to Noelle's chagrin, the conversation quickly turned to SPARK. Sam set up a large chart on the chalk ledge of the blackboard. The visual aid listed a side-by-side comparison of SPARK's beliefs with Christianity. Sam used a pointer as he read the points off the chart in a dry and uninspiring presentation.

Julia Beems finally cut in. "Excuse me, Sam, but this cult sounds like it has some really weird ideas. Nobody in their right mind would believe that silly stuff."

"It's all in the eye of the beholder," said Noelle. "You have to admit, our church has some strange sounding dogma, such as following a man who was killed and buried but then came back to life."

Christopher Kloss, out of his Santa suit and in a regular shirt and pants, chuckled. "Sounds like you're a fan of this group, Noelle."

"I don't agree with what they believe," she explained, "but I think we should be fair and not judge before we learn the facts. I mean, they're a little like us. They're looking for a place to belong and something that brings them comfort."

"I know enough about the cult to know that they're a bad influence on our youth," said Edna Apple, the schoolteacher. "Today my class was asking about the hippies. The kids thought living in a bus and doing nothing all day sounded like fun. I had my hands full trying to explain why they needed to stay in school and get an education. I told my students it's better to work hard instead of running away and goofing off."

Noelle turned to the mayor. "Chris, have the devotees caused any problems since they've arrived?"

He wrinkled his forehead. "Technically, they haven't broken any laws. As long as they stay put and mind their own business, I think we can safely ignore them."

"Let's get back on track," Sam said. "The point is that cults have heretical and possibly dangerous ideologies."

Noelle said, "I've met the devotees and they're not bad people at all."

Some of the people in the group gasped. Sam raised his eyebrows in shock. "You actually met them?"

"Yeah, and the mayor did too."

Sam stepped toward Noelle. "What are they like?"

She grinned. "They have horns, forked tongues, six arms and pointed tails. When they speak, fire shoots out of their mouths."

The group laughed. Sam set his mouth in a firm line and his eyes shot daggers at Noelle. But before he could reply, Trevor rushed into the room and dropped into the empty chair beside Noelle.

"Sorry I'm late," Trevor said. "Been busy at the office. What are we talking about tonight?"

"We were discussing the SPARK cult," said Sam.

"SPARK?" Trevor's eyes lit up. "What a coincidence. I was just working on a story—"

Noelle kicked him in the shin. Trevor glared at her. Noelle gave him a little shake of her hand, hoping the others in the circle didn't notice her signal.

"What kind of story?" May Wells asked.

Trevor opened his mouth but Noelle kicked him a second time. "Just a little something about their lifestyle. Right, Trevor?"

Someone passed by the open hallway door and rang a handbell to signal the end of the evening program. The group members stood up and put on their coats and jackets.

Chris said to Trevor, "I'm sure we're all looking forward to reading your story in the *Herald* tomorrow."

Sam tried to squeeze in some last-minute comments, but the people had stopped listening to him and instead were chatting with one other. Noelle started to go, but Trevor grabbed her arm and held her back as the others left the room.

When they were alone, he snapped. "What gives? My leg's black and blue from you walloping me."

"I didn't want you to spill the beans about Blossom."

"So what? The good folks of Yuletide need to wake up and see there's a world out there beyond their garage sales and lodge meetings."

"Yeah, and when the good folk hear that Blossom died of drugs, they'll march on the devotees with torches and pitchforks."

"It wouldn't be as bad as that, Noelle. The only time Yuletide ever came close to a mob riot was in 1944 when the town's finances came up short during the war and the mayor threatened to cancel the Fourth of July fireworks."

"But they might insist that the devotees leave town before we find out what really happened to the poor girl."

"What do you mean, *we*?"

The janitor, on his way down the hall, stopped by the doorway. "Time to lock up, folks."

"Thanks, we were just leaving," Trevor said.

Trevor snapped off the room light as he and Noelle left the room. They made their way through the basement's labyrinth of hallways and up the stairs to the outside door.

Noelle resumed the conversation. "I just had a thought. What if Blossom was killed by a religious fanatic? Someone who was convinced that SPARK is the devil's spawn? Someone who's trying to kill off the group one by one?"

"I think you're stretching it. I can't think of anyone in town who's that nutty."

"I do. There's a little church called True Believers Congregation that just started up on Pinecone Street. You must have heard of them. They've been running ads in the *Herald*."

"Sorry. I don't pay attention to what the advertising department does."

"Don't you read the paper once it's printed?"

"Only my articles."

"You're hopeless."

In the narthex, they joined the last group of stragglers leaving the building. Trevor pushed open one of the double entry doors and allowed Noelle to leave first. They walked down the concrete steps to the parking lot. Under the glow of the tall lights lining the lot, Trevor walked Noelle to her car, which was parked at the far end of the property.

"Look, Noelle," he said. "I know you mean well, but you should let the police handle the investigation."

"That's the trouble. There won't be an investigation. Whitlock is convinced the girl died of a self-inflicted overdose, and he'll leave it at that."

"You keep nosing around and you're gonna get yourself into some pretty deep hot water."

"What do you mean? As soon as the police chief sees your story in the paper tomorrow, he'll get moving."

Trevor pursed his lips. "Oh. Yes. About that." He paused as a family passed them on the way to their station wagon. "Look, Noelle, it's getting late and I'm beat. I'll talk to you tomorrow."

"Is something wrong?" she asked. "Is it about your story?"

But Trevor was already hurrying to his car at the other end of the lot.

Noelle pulled her open coat around herself against the cool night air. She wanted to follow the reporter and talk, but she, too, was exhausted and emotionally drained. Maybe it was best that they both get some rest and clear their heads.

On the drive home, Noelle switched on the radio that was always set to the Riverbend rock and roll station. As The Beatles' "Think for Yourself" played over the car speaker, she pondered why she was so interested in helping the group. She hardly knew Blossom. She had no connection with the devotees. She and SPARK had completely different worldviews. But still, Noelle hated to see anyone, regardless of who they were, treated unfairly. Every murder victim deserved justice, and nobody else wanted to solve the case.

At home, Noelle changed into her pajamas and settled on the sofa to read her mail and the newspaper. Ceebee jumped in her lap and she absently petted him. Blossom's killer was most likely someone connected with SPARK. The devotees seemed to be together all the time. An outsider would need to make a strong effort to pull Blossom away from the others. Maybe Noelle couldn't get close enough to interrogate First Sage, but she knew someone who could.

She picked up the Princess phone and soon had Dash Hanover on the line. She told him about SPARK and Blossom's death. He was reluctant to assist.

"Why not?" she said. "You helped me find the murderer of the stranger who came to my door."

"That was a different situation," Hanover said. "That man had a direct role in a SIAMESE mission. This girl means nothing to us."

"Look, Ceebee is still wearing his radio collar. And tomorrow SPARK is holding a big rally in Riverbend. Can we get Ceebee close to First Sage and Wise One? We might hear something about Blossom."

"I appreciate your fervor, Miss McNabb, but we have to prioritize our resources. We can't chase after every unsolved mystery."

"I know, but listen. In the past few weeks, we've had two murders here in town, which is two more killings than in the entire history of Yuletide. Don't you find that suspicious? The first murder had something to do with spies. And now, Old Scratch turns up at the same time as the SPARK group and we have another killing. Don't you think there might be a connection?"

"You believe SPARK may be a front for espionage?" A pause. "Let me do some checking and I'll get back to you tonight."

Hanover hung up. As much as Noelle wanted to crawl under the warm covers of her four-poster bed, she was determined to stay up long enough for Dash's reply. She made a snack of peanut butter toast to keep her awake, and turned on her black-and-white TV. She was too tired to dig out the weekly *TV Guide*, so she clicked the channel dial to check out the three networks. NBC had just started running *I Spy*. Noelle didn't need another stupid spy show. She had enough intrigue in her life. She settled on watching *The Danny Kaye Show* instead. At ten o'clock came the evening news with her cousin and favorite forecaster, Mamie Sprinkle. The weather girl had just finished her funny but accurate presentation when the phone rang.

"Our research people found some interesting correlations," said Hanover. "It appears that Old

Scratch and the SPARK cult are frequently present in the same cities simultaneously."

"So, the agent might be one of the SPARK people?"

"Not necessarily, but it's worth investigating. In our work, few occurrences are accidents."

He set a time tomorrow for Noelle and Destiny—and Ceebee—to go undercover.

Chapter 10: I Love the Flower Girl
Thursday

Bright and early the next day, Noelle threw on her robe and sneakers so she could run down the long gravel driveway to Ornament Lane and the paper box—a plastic box nailed to the wooden post that held the two metal mailboxes, one each for herself and the landlords—to retrieve the newest edition of the *Yuletide Herald*. She flipped through the pages, eager to read Trevor's article on Blossom—and found nothing. Nothing? Not one word about the devotees on any page.

The paper, however, did contain a full-page color advertisement paid for by the True Believers Congregation. Noelle scanned the long ad message that berated SPARK for leading people away from the Gospel and for promoting sin and evil. How could the paper run such hate? Noelle was determined to write a letter to the editor or, better yet, drop in on the *Herald* office to give those in charge a piece of her mind.

In the meantime, she gulped down a quick breakfast—a bowl of Lucky Charms cold cereal with milk, orange juice and half a grapefruit—and wrestled a feisty Ceebee into his carrier. If Hanover wanted the cat for any more missions, he'd have to find a better way of hauling the animal to and fro. Noelle drove herself and her pet to the hippie pad, actually a farm outside the Yuletide city limits where Moonbaby and Rambler lived along with their livestock and dogs. Noelle parked outside the rustic, two-story house the hippies called home.

Moments later, Destiny arrived in a van painted in psychedelic colors. Destiny got out and shooed away the yappy dogs that rushed her. She was decked out as a bohemian with knee-length, lace-up leather boots; a miniskirt; colorful print tunic with flared long sleeves; bracelets and a felt beret atop a wig of black cornrows.

"Wow!" said Noelle. "You look fantastic! And you can't tell me that's an official SIAMESE company vehicle."

"It's our phone repair van. The garage crew repainted the outside."

"I thought we were going to be inconspicuous."

"We are. Our new wheels are in style for a freak-out."

Destiny took a box off the passenger seat and followed Noelle inside the house. They met Moonbaby in the living room, which was filled with secondhand furniture, flowerpots suspended from the ceiling in macramé holders, pop art paintings and beanbag chairs. The scent of sandalwood incense hung in the air. Noelle introduced the spy to her friend.

"Hey, what's happening?" said Moonbaby. "You're lookin' pretty groovy."

Density nodded and set her box on the wood-plank table. Noelle placed the pet carrier beside the box and the cat yowled.

"That must be Ceebee," Moonbaby observed. "So, Noelle, you called and said you wanted me to doll you up as a hippie?"

"That's right," said Noelle. "I figured if anyone could do it, it had to be you."

"So, let's go look at some threads. But first, go wash your face. Hippies let their natural glow shine."

Noelle obediently stepped in the bathroom and scrubbed the makeup off her face at the porcelain sink. Then she followed Moonbaby upstairs to the cluttered bedroom. They rummaged through a huge closet full of clothes. Moonbaby was a larger size than thin Noelle, so most of the pieces didn't fit. But with a needle and thread, Moonbaby altered some of the clothes for a better fit. Noelle ended up wearing a short-sleeved, tie-dyed shirt with a long, colorful scarf draped over her neck along with sandals, bell bottoms embroidered with doves and flowers, and a leather jacket covered in numerous pins depicting a peace sign, The Beatles and slogans like "Ban the Bomb" and "War is Not Healthy for Children and Other Living Things."

"I'll bring these clothes back as soon as I'm done with them," said Noelle.

"Naw, keep them," said the hippie. "It's too much effort for me to size them back the way they were."

They rejoined Destiny in the living room, where the spy had been inspecting a framed Andy Warhol print hung on a wall. Destiny opened the box she had brought and removed a wig of long black hair.

She nodded at Noelle. "Park your butt and I'll put this on you."

Noelle sat down on a straight-back chair. Destiny stood behind her and fitted the wig over her short brown hair.

Moonbaby popped a floppy-brim cloth hat over the wig. "Ain't that a gasser! You should keep that look."

"And put these on." Destiny handed Noelle a pair of eyeglasses that had also been packed in the box.

Noelle held the earpieces and inspected the tinted, rectangular lens. "Is this really necessary?"

"If we run into the Yuletide gang, we don't want them to recognize you," said Destiny.

Noelle slipped the thin, curved earpieces over each ear. She squinted through the colored lens. "I always wanted to look at the world through rose-colored glasses."

Destiny took a metal comb from the box and handed it to Noelle.

"Thanks, but I don't think I need it," said the recipient.

"Sure, you do. It's a radio." Destiny demonstrated. The "beads" along the side of the comb were actually buttons to turn it on and off. "While you're out in the field with acoustic kitty, I'll be in the van. This is how we'll talk."

"SIAMESE thinks of everything, don't they?"

"If they didn't, we'd be dead."

Moonbaby added one final touch to Noelle's outfit. She mixed some watercolors and painted a cat face on Noelle's left cheek. She gave her a hand mirror so she could view the results.

"Moonbaby, I love it! I'll never wash it off."

The hippie gave one last piece of advice. "And ditch your watches. Hippies show up on their own time."

The women dutifully removed their wristwatches. Destiny put her timepiece in a pocket; Noelle placed her watch and the comb in the large leather handbag she had brought from home.

"Come on, let's go, so I can nail a good parking spot near the target," said Destiny.

"Wait, before you split." Moonbaby dug out an old Kodak camera. "You girls are so fab. Rambler just loaded a new roll of film last night. Lemme take your picture."

"No! No pictures!" Destiny snatched the camera away.

"Hey, chill," said Moonbaby.

"Our identities must remain secret."

"I won't tell no one."

"Photos have a way of getting out where you don't want someone to see them."

"Okay, I dig. I won't snap your mugs. Can I have my camera back?"

Destiny set the Kodak on the table and ran out of the house before Moonbaby could pick up the camera and sneak in a quick shot. Noelle thanked the hippie for her help, grabbed Ceebee's carrier and left. As Destiny drove, she reviewed the plan with Noelle. First, they'd mingle with the crowd and see if they might pick up some information about Blossom. The rally was expected to attract people from throughout the tri-state area—Indiana, Illinois and Kentucky—so the women had a good chance of meeting someone who might have known the dead girl. After working the crowd, they'd locate the target: Wise One and First Sage. Noelle would release Ceebee while Destiny monitored the radio pickup from the van. They'd clear out before the rally began.

The park was already filling up when they pulled in. Destiny circled the area until Noelle spotted the Cadillac that First Sage had used in Yuletide. Beside the car stood a Ford truck with a metal camper hooked up behind it.

"Bingo!" Destiny parked the van behind some trees near the camper. "That looks like a good place for Wise One to cool his heels in private."

"Yeah, but if the targets are inside, Ceebee won't be much good on the outside."

"My guess is they'll come outside eventually. Anyone inside that dinky camper will get cabin fever. Let's go mix with the guests."

Noelle opened the carrier and dumped Ceebee on her lap.

Destiny stared at the animal. "You gonna haul that fat cat around the park?"

"He'll whine if I leave him here alone. Don't worry; Ceebee won't run away. He doesn't mix with strangers. Besides, people like to talk to folks with pets."

They left the van and headed past the trees into a large, open grassy area that spread across some low hills. The weather was perfect for the rally—cool but clear, sunny and blue skies with no rain in the forecast, according to Mamie's weather prediction the night before. The crowd consisted mostly young people in their 20s and 30s who were dressed casually in denim, leather pants, tee-shirts and overalls. A cluster of beatniks in all-black shirts and pants smoked thin, foreign cigars and eyed the passers-by. SPARK devotees in their sandals and blue robes were making their way through the mob, passing out pamphlets and priming the guests for the talks to come. Noelle recognized some devotees from the Yuletide group and avoided them. Uniformed policemen were scattered throughout, scanning the people intently through their mirrored sunglasses. After the recent wave of local demonstrations against the Vietnam War, the cops were wary of all large crowds of counterculture radicals.

Nearby was the natural amphitheater. At the base of a hollow stood the stage; rows of concrete benches were built into the hillside. In the middle of the stage stood a raised throne where the Wise One would impart his enlightened thoughts. Other chairs stood on either side of the throne. Behind the chairs rose aluminum poles that held silk banners with pictures of birds and flowers surrounding the words "love," "joy," "peace," "harmony," "oneness" and "wisdom."

Destiny and Noelle split up to mix with the guests. Noelle caught the eye of some people and smiled at them, but they either ignored her or gave a brief nod of acknowledgement before moving on. She was dying to start asking about Blossom, but she didn't want to frighten people with her eagerness.

A devotee that Noelle didn't know, a pretty girl with long wavy hair, approached and started to hand her a brochure. "Ooh! What a pretty cat!"

"His name is Ceebee. Would you like to pet him?" Noelle spoke slowly and in a lower pitch in an effort to disguise her voice.

"May I?" The girl stroked the cat's back. The animal eyed her but the petting kept him calm. "What is that thing around his neck?"

Noelle thought fast. "It's a brace to keep his neck straight. He had an operation."

"Oh, the poor creature."

"But he's doing better now. What's your name, and do you live around here?"

"I'm Skye, and I go wherever Wise One tells me to go."

"Where are you from originally? Where did you grow up?"

"Before I was enlightened, I used to live in a little town in Illinois."

What luck! Maybe the devotee lived near Blossom's hometown. Noelle struggled to keep her enthusiasm down. "I knew a devotee who lived in Homestead, Illinois. Homestead's in the northern part of Illinois. I don't suppose you know anyone from there?"

The girl scrunched up her face in concentration. "I'm not sure. I think so. Let me go and ask."

She vanished into a crowd of followers, and soon returned, pulling along a young man with shoulder-length blond hair and wearing a blue robe. "This is Fillmore. He's from Homestead."

"I'm Starshine," said Noelle. "I knew a girl from Homestead. When she became a devotee, she called herself Blossom."

"Blossom?" said Fillmore. "Was that the girl who died yesterday?"

"You heard about that?"

"Yes, it was very, very sad," said Skye.

"Yeah, I knew her," said Fillmore. "She went to my high school. We didn't hang out together, but I knew her. Back then she was called Janet Campbell."

Noelle shifted Ceebee in her arms. The heavy feline was cramping her muscles. "She was a nice girl. I bet she had a lot of friends."

"No, not really," he said. "Kinda a loner. I hear she had a pagan boyfriend. He didn't like her dumping him for the Wise One."

"Did that make him mad?"

"Yeah, he was pretty bummed," said Fillmore. "He said he'd get her out of SPARK if he had to drag her out by her hair."

Someone bumped against Noelle. She turned to see the back of a woman, dressed in a denim jacket and blue jeans, walking away. The stranger hurried by without even an "excuse me."

She returned her attention to Fillmore. "What was his name? The boyfriend?"

"Go ask him. That's him over there." The devotee pointed to a tall, stocky man standing off in the distance beneath an oak tree. "I'm guessing he came here looking for Blossom."

Or maybe he had found her at the campgrounds the day before, and killed her when she refused to leave with him.

Noelle asked, "What's his name?"

Skye stared at the leather purse hanging over Noelle's shoulder. "Is your bag beeping?"

Indeed, a low but clear pulsing sound was emanating from inside the satchel. Noelle blushed. "It's, ah, it's a timer. Yeah, it's a little alarm clock. Time to give my cat some medicine. Will you excuse me, please?"

The two devotees waved as Noelle scurried off. "Hope you enjoy the rally! Blessings!"

Drat! Of all the bad luck. The first decent clue about Blossom's death, but she couldn't get a name. Maybe she and Destiny could track down the boyfriend later—unless he left the park early. Noelle sat down on a bench away from the crowd and deposited Ceebee on the seat beside her. She put the handbag on her lap and took out the SIAMESE comb. A red "bead" on the comb handle was flashing as the beeping continued. Noelle glanced around, but no one was looking her way. She pulled the short wire antenna from the comb and pretended to brush her wig. She pressed a green bead to talk and released it to listen.

She leaned her face over the comb and whispered. "Tabby Gray calling Black Manx."

"Speak up, I can barely hear you," Destiny said.

"Sorry. I don't want anyone to hear me."

"You're supposed to find a secluded place to talk."

"This is all I can find."

"All right, shut up and I'll talk. The people inside the camper opened the door. If the cat sits outside the door, the mic will pick up their voices."

"But Destiny, I found a guy who might be responsible for Blossom's death."

"We don't have time for that. The mission takes priority. Get the cat over here pronto."

Noelle sighed. "Right. On my way."

One of the beatniks was staring at Noelle. She began combing her hair and singing loudly. Noelle waved at the man and he moved away. She stuffed the comb into her bag, slung the strap over a shoulder, scooped up Ceebee, and walked briskly toward the camper. Once Noelle had Ceebee in place, she had no reason to stay near the target. Destiny didn't need her inside the van. Noelle could have a quick chat with the ex-boyfriend while Ceebee was doing his job.

Noelle approached the target. No one was looking out the white-curtain-covered windows of the camper. So far, so good. She stepped over the twigs on the ground to avoid making a sound. She hid behind a tree just a few yards from the silver vehicle.

Noelle set the cat on the ground and gave him a treat. "Okay, Ceebee, see the camper? Go to the steps and stay. Stay at the steps."

She tossed a treat near the camper and pushed the pet in that direction. Ceebee started off and turned around. Noelle threw out another treat in the direction of the vehicle. The cat ran to the treat, gobbled it up, and continued waddling to the camper. He started to climb the steps. Noelle realized she had no microphone for communicating with the cat. Ceebee jumped up the stairs and hurried into the camper. Noelle sniffed the air and realized why Ceebee was acting peculiar—someone inside the vehicle was cooking chicken soup. The cat must have smelled the savory aroma too. And if the people inside the camper saw the cat and the collar—

Chapter 11: Don't Let Me Be Misunderstood

Noelle dug the comb out of her pouch and turned it on. "Destiny, mayday! Ceebee is inside the camper!"

The spy's voice crackled over the tiny speaker inside the comb handle. "What! Why did you let him do that?"

"I didn't tell him to go there. And I can't talk to him and tell him to leave."

"Hang on."

Seconds later, Ceebee came bounding out of the camper, flying down the steps and running toward Noelle. She grabbed him as he tried to dart past her.

Destiny's voice came over the comb radio. "Did it work?"

"Did what work?"

"I radioed a high-pitched squeal through the cat's earpiece. I figured that might frighten him."

"It sure did. He almost ran out of the park. Now I have to convince him to go back to the camper."

She petted the cat for a moment until he stopped shaking. Then she put Ceebee back on the ground, gave him another treat, and threw another goodie at the target. If this kept up, Noelle might run out of treats, plus the cat would grow too fat to fit in the collar. Ceebee trotted back to the camper, snatched up the treat, and stopped at the base of the stairs. He glanced up at the steps and, perhaps remembering his previous shocking experience, stretched out on the ground below the open door. Good.

Noelle turned on her comb. "Ceebee is in place. He's settled. I'm going back to the rally to check on the suspect."

"Noelle! You can't leave!"

"Ceebee is doing fine. I'll only be away a few minutes."

She turned off the comb before Destiny could object further. With Ceebee resting comfortably, Noelle ran back to the grassy area. By now, more people had arrived, and the devotees were more aggressive in their evangelizing. Blossom's former beau wasn't where Noelle had seen him earlier. Did he leave the park? Noelle pushed her way through the mob, aware of the minutes ticking by. The comb beeped. Noelle removed her scarf, reached into the bag, and wrapped the scarf around the comb to muffle the sound. She resumed her search, moving farther away from the camper. Noelle was ready to give up when she spotted the ex-boyfriend. Unlike most of the crowd, he wore regular clothes: tan trousers, shirt and a windbreaker with the hood pulled up over his head. He was talking to a lovely young lady about Blossom's age. Did the cad have a new girlfriend already? She looked stunning in black slacks and a pink, vee-neck pullover of mohair.

"Hi, there! Can I cut in?" Noelle sounded cheerful, which was considerable acting on her part, as she wanted to immediately grill the man about the murder.

He glared at her. "We're busy. Go away."

"Only take a minute."

"Who are you? What do you want?"

"I'm a friend of Blossom. Heard she was a friend of yours."

"Blossom? Who's that?"

"You probably know her better as Janet Campbell."

"Oh, her. What about her?"

"I heard you had a thing for her."

"Yeah, so what if I did? That's all over now, baby. She went her way and I went mine."

"You didn't hear what happened to her?"

"Freddie, who's this Janet Campbell?" asked the man's girlfriend.

"Nobody special, just a chick I knew back home," said Freddie. "She ran off with a bunch of freakazoids."

"If you think they're strange," Noelle asked, "why are you here at the rally?"

"I got family in Riverbend," he said. "I came to see my folks, and my friend here wanted to check out the scene."

The girl gave Noelle a smile and a wave.

Freddie started to move away. "We're ready to split, so we'll be seeing you."

"Wait!" said Noelle. "You haven't heard that Blossom—I mean Janet—is dead?"

Freddie's face contorted in—what? Rage, sorrow or surprise? Noelle couldn't read his emotions. "Dead?"

"Dead?" the girlfriend echoed. "Freddie, what's this all about?"

"Beats me," he replied. "I guess all the plants and shrubs those oddballs eat isn't too healthy."

"She died of a drug overdose," said Noelle. "Probably heroin. The police think someone forced the drugs on her." Noelle knew that wasn't true, but she wanted to see Freddie's reaction.

"If you're trying to pin something on me, girlie, forget it," he said. "I haven't seen Janet since she left me. My girl and I just breezed into this hick town this morning."

"He's right," his companion affirmed. "We've been on the road all night. We drove straight through Illinois. We stopped for lunch at McDonald's and here we are."

"Sorry. I wasn't accusing you of anything," said Noelle. "Just thought you'd like to know."

"Okay, so now I know," said Freddie. "I told Janet not to get hung up with these jokers. Too bad for her. Now we really gotta split, miss—I never got your name."

"I never gave it." Noelle hurried away. If she stayed and questioned him further, Freddie might get suspicious and call for a policeman.

Since Noelle wasn't carrying her fat cat, she could move fast. Noelle bypassed the crowds via a shortcut through the trees. She ran to the camper and stopped at her former hiding place—just in time to see a man walk down the camper stairs and step on Ceebee's tail.

The cat yowled and shot off into the trees. Noelle chased the cat, shoving her way through the dense woods and not caring how much noise she made. She shouted for Ceebee to stop. The tinted glasses made it difficult to see as the thick overhead branches cut out the sunlight. The lower branches slapped her face as she ran. Ceebee darted out of the woods and onto the grass behind the amphitheater stage. Noelle broke out of the trees and grabbed the cat. To her right, technicians were on the stage, setting up microphones for the speakers. People were finding seats on the benches. On Noelle's left ran a creek, swollen by the recent rains. The banners hanging at the back of the stage hid her from the audience. She heard voices behind her and turned.

Two men were walking down the dirt patch that led from the camper and through the woods. First Sage, in his gold robe, strode beside a man Noelle had not met, but whom she recognized from photos in the SPARK brochures. The Wise One looked unimpressive, not what one might expect from the leader of an infamous cult. Noelle was struck by how short he was, especially since he was stooped over; the top of Wise One's head just reached the shoulder of his aide. He tottered on in quick but short, careful steps. Thin wisps of white hair tried to escape from beneath a red turban. The long multi-colored robe hung loosely over his thin body. His boney arms were lost in the folds of the long sleeves. Wise One's wrinkled face belied his age. Liver spots coved the back of his hands. Yet his tiny, close-set eyes glowed with an inner light.

Noelle didn't have time to ponder what made this man so special that people left their homes to follow him. If she stood still or ran back into the trees, the men would see her. If she went the other direction, the people in the amphitheater would spot her. Where to go? Noelle turned to her left and darted for the creek. The water appeared deep enough to hide her.

Just as Noelle jumped off the bank, a thought flashed by: Cat collar. Wires. Water. Electrocution. In mid-air she flung Ceebee back over her shoulder, trusting in his ability to land on all four feet. She took a deep gulp of air and closed her eyes seconds before landing in the cold, dirty water. Once over the shock of the chilly water, Noelle let the current carry her downstream and away from the stage area. She kept her head beneath the surface until her air ran out. Noelle poked her head up out of the water. She'd drifted far enough downstream that the folks at the rally wouldn't see her. With her long legs, her feet just touched the bottom of the creek. She waded to the bank and climbed out, a soggy mess. Noelle shook her head and limbs in an attempt to dry off. Ceebee trotted toward her, fussing but dry.

She picked him up. "Come on, you little acoustic kitty. Time for you to retire from spy work."

Noelle passed behind the banners on the amphitheater stage and quickly reached the dirt path that led through the woods. By now First Sage and Wise One were on the stage; they never saw her or the cat. Noelle soon reached the SIAMESE van. She rapped on the back door, two long knocks and three short, the prearranged signal.

Destiny opened the back door and gasped. "Girl, what in blazes happened to you?"

"Thought I'd take a little swim. Can we come in?"

Density took Ceebee from her hands and deposited him on a chair. Then she took Noelle's hands and pulled her up into the vehicle.

"I need to dry off," Noelle said.

The spy opened a metal bin and took out a blanket. "Use this. Comes in handy during those cold Hoosier winters."

Noelle wrapped the blanket around her, picked up Ceebee, and sat down in the chair. She removed the tinted glasses and blinked, grateful to once again see clearly. Destiny rewound the reel on the tape machine.

"So did the eavesdropping work?" Noelle said.

"Like a charm."

Noelle inspected the cat collar. "Uh oh."

"Now what?"

"The collar's rubbing his skin raw. See? Ceebee's got a big red sore on his neck."

Destiny opened a compartment in the console and removed a key, which she used to unlock the collar. The metal ring fell apart for easy removal.

Noelle said, "You mean you could have taken off the collar at any time?"

"Yeah, but we have to recalibrate the microphone every time we put it back on." Destiny placed the key and the collar into the compartment and shut it. "I'll take this to headquarters and see if Dr. Albedo can make it more comfy."

"Yeah, put some padding on it or something."

"What was that awful racket at the end of the tape? Sounded like the cat was strangled."

"Someone stepped on his tail." Noelle described her adventure at the creek.

Destiny fussed with the tape machine. "In future, we need a listening device that doesn't roam. Did you get a look at the men who left the camper?"

"That's easy. They were First Sage and Wise One. Didn't you see them with the van camera?"

Destiny shook her head. "The camera can't see through walls or trees."

"So, what did they talk about?"

Destiny pressed the play button on the machine, and the tape played over a small speaker.

Noelle said, "That's First Sage, definitely him." Next came a high pitched, child-like voice, soft and squeaky. "Is that the Wise One?" She giggled. "I'd never expect the leader of a cult to sound like that!"

"Quiet!" said Destiny.

On the tape the two cult leaders discussed finances. First Sage was worried that the group was running low on money to pay for their expenses at the Yuletide campgrounds.

"You are too concerned with material woes," said Wise One. "Have faith. I have been informed that we have large donations on the way." He named a well-known rock musician who had become enamored with SPARK and had promised a considerable contribution.

"That's funny," said Noelle. "At the record store I keep up on all the pop music news. That particular singer has never said a word about SPARK."

Destiny shushed her as the tape continued through the machine's rollers.

"Are you certain of this?" First Sage asked.

"Oh, yes. Mac has assured me of such."

"But we need money now, not sometime in the future."

Wise One assured him that they were bound to raise enough funds at the rally today.

"And what if we don't?" First Sage asked. "Feeding the devotees is costing a great deal, and we are no longer allowed to solicit the residents of Yuletide. They're treading on our First Amendment rights. We could sue them."

"Oh, no, no, no, no," said Wise One. "Please, no court battles. Such unpleasantness. We represent love and peace, not strife and conflict. We do not wish to have the public see us as troublemakers."

"You are right as always, Wise One," said First Sage. "As we must also not let word get out about the death of the girl."

Noelle perked up. They were finally talking about Blossom. What did they know about her demise?

"That poor child," said Wise One. "We must give her the proper ritual as her spirit makes its way to the forever domain. That is only right."

"The family wants us to return the body to them for a pagan burial," said First Sage.

"Such bad news," said Wise One. "Is it true that she died of drugs?"

"I don't know, Wise One. I pray not, but the evidence seemed clear."

"Dear me. We must work harder with the children. Teach them not to partake of harmful substances. You will make that a priority in your lessons."

"Yes, Wise One, of course."

"And we must keep her manner of death quiet. That would only cause anxiety and fear among the children. They must see us as a place of safety, not danger."

"Yes, I have only stated that the girl died of sickness."

"Good, good, that is best."

Destiny pressed the machine's stop button. "Now we see the real cult. Love and light on the outside, with a dark underbelly. Wonder what other secrets they have?"

"What else does the tape say?" Noelle asked.

"Not much." Destiny hit the rewind button. "That's all they say about the girl. The rest is Wise One going over his talk for the rally."

"If they're covering up the cause of Blossom's death, that means SPARK is responsible somehow."

"Not necessarily." Destiny removed the full reel from the machine and placed it in a cardboard box that she labeled with a felt marker. "Dead members are bad for their recruiting efforts." She put the box in a drawer. "The bad news is they didn't talk about espionage operations, which was the whole point of us being here."

"Maybe they covered that before we started listening in."

"I don't sense that either one of them is Old Scratch, especially not the old coot. They wouldn't be putting on an act in private. Our work here is done. I'm beat. Let's beat it."

The women and the cat got into the cab and headed back to Yuletide.

Noelle broke the silence. "So, you still think it's a coincidence that Old Scratch and SPARK showed up together in the same towns?"

"I think we're barking up the wrong tree with that group." With one hand on the wheel, Destiny yanked off her wig with her other hand and shook her head to fluff her afro. "Ahhh, that's better. Before acoustic cat got in place, I nosed around the stage with the city bigwigs who were setting up for the rally. The people I talked to seemed to think SPARK was a legit group, a little wacky, but sincere. First

116 Hippie Haven Homicide

Sage paid cash to rent the park for the day. All the permit paperwork he filled out passed the smell test. If there's any dirt on SPARK, they've swept it under a rug."

Noelle put Ceebee into the carrier—he went in easily, happy to be in a safe and cozy place away from strangers. As they cruised the highway, Noelle related her conversation with Freddie.

"Ordinarily I'd chew you out for leaving your post, but I'll let it slide," said Destiny. "What do you think? Was he lying?"

"I don't know. He seemed adamant that he didn't do it. But I'm still green about reading people. I don't have your sixth sense about truth telling."

"That's 'cause you've live a sheltered life in your little Christmas town. You haven't met enough of the scum yet."

Noelle shot her buddy a look. "But why did he turn up in Riverbend the day after she died?"

"Hate to interrupt your sleuthing, but we got bigger fish to fry. There's still the matter of Old Scratch."

"Oh yeah, him." Noelle wasn't enthused about the change of topic. The death of a friend meant more to her than a faceless Cold War spy.

Destiny continued. "If we can't get close to Old Scratch, we need to make him come to us. Flush him out in the open."

"How do we do that?"

"He's in the market for secrets. If we dangle the right kind of bait, he might bite."

"Bait? You mean we pretend we have secrets to buy or sell?"

"Not real ones, of course. We're not stupid. But we can offer some fake goodies he'd love to have. Something tasty he can't get anywhere else."

"How do we contact him? Put an ad in the newspaper?"

"Don't worry. We'll think of something." Destiny pulled in front of the hippie pad outside the Yuletide city limits and parked beside Noelle's Bug. "Here's your stop. Go home and have lunch. We'll be in touch."

"Lunch. That reminds me. Someone inside the camper was cooking chicken soup. That's why Ceebee went inside the RV. He smelled it too."

"So what?"

"The devotees are vegetarians. Why would they want chicken soup?"

"Maybe First Sage and Wise Ones are fakers after all. They slip in some meat on the side."

"Or maybe a third person was in the camper with them."

Chapter 12: Young Girl Blues

Destiny stared at Noelle. "We only picked up two voices on the tape."

"Maybe the other guy was sleeping or reading the newspaper or in the bathroom. Maybe his voice didn't carry far enough for the microphone to pick up. Wise One did mention someone named Mac."

"Good point. I'll see if our files have anyone called Mac, although that sounds like an alias if I ever heard one." Destiny pressed a button that automatically opened the passenger door. "Okay, pop out. I need to shoot back to HQ before Dash sends out a posse to look for me."

"What about the comb and the wig and the glasses?"

"Keep it. You might need them again soon. And put some ointment on the cat's neck. The poor thing looks like a possum bit him."

Noelle wanted to talk more, but SIAMESE agents ran on their own timetable. She climbed out of the cab. Destiny shut the van door by remote control and, without a goodbye, floored the pedal and roared away. Soon Noelle had driven back to her cottage. She rubbed some Bactine Medicated Skin Cream on the raw spot on the cat's neck. Ceebee fussed at the medicine's sting, but he quickly forgave her and sat on his rump to wash his face. Noelle opened the door, and Ceebee darted outside and ran freely across the lawn, happy to be back in his domain and rid of the bulky collar that had dragged him down.

With Ceebee out of the way, Noelle took a Mr. Bubble bath to clean up and relax. She hated to wash off the cat "tattoo" on her face, but scrubbed it anyway. In her bathrobe and slippers, she retired to the living room, sat on the sofa and began to unload the items from her leather shoulder bag. She found something she hadn't put in—a folded piece of paper. Inside the paper, she found a dollar bill torn in half along with a note that read:

To learn more about your dead friend, meet me at Lollypop Lanes tonight seven o'clock. Look for other half of bill.

No signature or name. The note was neatly printed with no exaggerated features that would help identify the writer. How did this get into the purse? Noelle remembered the woman who had bumped into her at the rally. Had the stranger overheard the conversation and slipped her the note? What did the snoop know about Blossom's death?

Lollypop Lanes, the town's only bowling alley, had a busy schedule of adult leagues during the week, children and teen leagues Saturday mornings and afternoons, and open bowling for non-league singles and families on Friday and Saturday nights. Sunday the lane was closed, as were most businesses in Yuletide. Thursdays began with a women's league in the morning and a coed group of retirees and their wives in the afternoon. The only league at play that evening was Roller Girls for 20-to-40-year-old women, mostly single but some married. Noelle still had the fourteen-pound ball and the bowling shoes she'd used when she was on a high school league. Noelle wouldn't look out of place among the league women if she dropped in.

Noelle carried her bowling bag into the alley at ten minutes to seven. She was dressed in a calf-length black shirt and slip, white ankle socks and flats, and a red polo shirt in place of her old league shirt. Would the contact still recognize her without her Starshine costume? But hippies didn't hang out at the lanes, and she wanted to blend in with the Thursday night crowd.

As Noelle pushed opened the glass door leading into the alley, she left the nighttime quiet for a cacophony of noise: pins falling, balls rolling down the lanes, women chattering, loudspeaker announcements and jukebox music. The odor of beer, buttered popcorn and sweat wafted through the space. In keeping with the Christmas theme of the town, green garlands were draped around the walls. Wreaths decorated with lollypops hung over the automatic pinsetters at the end of each lane. The interior color scene was in bright primary colors of red, green and blue. The male staff that took care of the equipment and gave the lessons wore standard bowling attires, but the female staff at the front counter and snack bar looked cute in their red faux-velvet blouses and skirts trimmed in white fur.

At the counter Noelle paid for a game—might look suspicious if she just stood around and waited for her connection. Noelle hurried past the busy lanes, avoiding eye contact lest she meet someone she knew who wanted to strike up a conversation. But the ladies were too occupied with their games to notice. The last four lanes on the right-hand side were open. Noelle staked out the lane nearest the wall. She placed her paper score sheet on the scoring table; a sharpened pencil was in place to record her pins. She draped her jacket over the back of the chair at the table. Then she sat on the modeled plastic bench to change into her red bowling shoes. She glanced around but saw no one unusual. Was the note simply a ruse to get her out of the house? Noelle threw her first frame. Ordinarily, she was a pretty good bowler, but she found it difficult to concentrate on the game. If no one showed up after she finished one game, she'd leave.

After bowling her fifth frame, a young woman about Blossom's age arrived at the third lane from the wall. She wore a black jacket, blank pants, a white blouse and sneakers. She carried rented shoes and a plain black house ball picked up from one of the ball racks. The stranger set her ball in the ball return and fussed with her score sheet. Noelle guessed that the girl didn't know what she was doing. Noelle sat at the table and doodled on her score sheet while watching the girl from the corner of her eye. After putting on her bowling shoes, the newcomer threw an awkward first ball by taking a few steps to the foul line and then bending over and tossing the ball forward with both hands. The ball limped down the lane and toppled into the gutter. The girl stood by the ball return with no reaction to the bad shot. She didn't mark her score sheet.

Noelle took the torn dollar from her purse and approached the bowler. "Excuse me, but you look thirsty. Would you like to buy yourself a drink from the refreshment bar?" She held out the bill.

The girl glanced at the money and then at Noelle. A smile eased across her face. She reached in her pants pocket and pulled out half of a dollar bill. The two pieces fit.

"Let's sit over here." Noelle motioned at the chairs behind her scoring table. Noelle had never seen the girl before. She was short, long dark hair, pug nose and on the plump side. Her eyes were wide with fear and anxiety.

They sat down. "Did the girl at the park send you?" The stranger talked so low that Noelle could barely hear her over the din of the league play.

"I am she. I was in disguise."

"Why?"

"That isn't important. What's your name?"

"Call me Marlo."

No last name. Noelle wondered if Marlo was her real first name. Should she also use an alias as well?

But if she wanted the girl to trust her, she'd better start with the truth. "I'm Noelle. This is an odd place for a meeting."

"I figured no one would hear us over the noise."

"Yeah, but it'll look strange if we're not bowling. Tell you what. I'll bowl and you sit at the table and keep score."

"I don't know how to do that."

"Just draw on the paper. The score doesn't matter. We'll talk between frames."

Marlo nodded and took her place at the table as Noelle picked up her ball for the next frame. She easily picked up a split with her second ball.

While waiting for the ball to return she sat beside Marlo. "Do you live around here?"

"Not anymore. I grew up in Yuletide. That's how I knew about the bowling alley. The place still looks the same. Nothing changes in Yuletide. But I know SPARK is here. They send out a newsletter every month with the cities they plan to visit. When I left SPARK, I got on the mailing list so I could keep tabs on Janet."

Noelle's eyebrows shot up. "You were in SPARK?"

"Yeah, for a while. That's how I met Janet. We were welcomed in about the same time. That's what they call their initiation—welcoming in."

The bowlers on the other lane were eyeing them, so Noelle got up and bowled again. This time she didn't make a spare. She wasn't thinking about the game; she just wanted to hear more of Marlo's tale.

Noelle resumed her seat beside Marlo. "SPARK just let you walk way?"

"Well, no. They don't like people leaving. But I'd had enough. I asked to go, but First Sage wouldn't hear of it. He told me to keep meditating and reading the Wise One's words and soon the truth of it would dawn on me. Yeah, right. I left one night when we were staying at a motel in Dayton, Ohio. When everyone was asleep, I jumped out of the window."

"And you survived?" Noelle asked.

"We were on the first floor. Anyway, I hitchhiked through Kentucky and Indiana until I reached Riverbend."

"Why were you at the rally?"

"I came to see Janet. Then someone told me she was dead. I just couldn't believe it. When I overheard you talking at the park, I thought you might be able to help."

"Excuse me, I need to bowl again." On the next frame—the eighth—Noelle made a strike. Marlo's tale was energizing her.

Noelle resumed her seat on the bench. "Why did you leave SPARK?"

"I just didn't get it. I didn't feel all warm inside like everyone else. It's all right for them, but the teaching didn't light any sparks in me. Janet got into it big time. She loved every minute of it. Except when she had that run-in at the office."

"Go on."

"Before Blossom—I mean, Janet—joined SPARK, she worked as a secretary, so sometimes First Sage asked her to do some clerical work, not much, just some light typing and stuffing envelopes. The secretaries handled the important letters and financial stuff. Janet was working in the Dayton office. One day she told me she'd found some locked file drawers in the office. She thought that was weird. We were told that SPARK is honest and has nothing to hide. She found a file folder on top of one of the locked cabinets. She looked inside the folder to see where to store it. Then a man came into the room and yelled at her and slapped her for looking at the file."

"That's terrible!"

"The man told Janet she was going to hell for her bad deed. She cried and said she'd never do it again. The man made her promise to never tell anyone about the locked files."

"Who was the man? First Sage?"

Marlo shook her head. "Oh, no. At least that's what Janet told me. Janet said she'd never seen him before. She didn't know his name. But he had to be someone who worked with SPARK. Nobody was allowed in the offices except First Sage and the secretaries."

"Did Janet ever tell First Sage about the man or the files?"

"We were all afraid of First Sage. He's kind and treats everyone well, but, well, there's something about him. Nobody talked about it, but everyone knew that you didn't want to cross First Sage. But maybe First Sage was the one who hit her. She might have lied about that."

"Someone hit Janet. Is that why you left?"

"I'd been unhappy for some time, but that did it. I couldn't stay there and watch my friend get beat up. I begged Janet to leave with me, but she wouldn't hear of it. She loved SPARK."

Noelle glanced up at the upper level. The manager of Lollypop Lanes was eyeing her, so she bowled again. As a result of rushing her play, she missed what should have been an easy spare. The manager moved on. Noelle returned to her seat, and Marlo resumed her tale.

"Did Janet see what was in the file?" Noelle asked.

"I think so, but she didn't tell me what it was. She just wanted to forget the whole thing and get back to the singing and playtime."

"Do you think this man might have wanted to kill Janet?" Marlo shrugged, so Noelle pressed on with another question. "Did Blossom have any enemies in her hometown? Someone in her past?"

"She didn't like her stepfamily. And she had this flakey boyfriend."

"Yeah, I've met him."

"Janet owed money to some people. That might be why she wanted to get out of town with SPARK."

"Was she in hock to a loan shark?"

"I don't know. When I was in SPARK, Janet seldom talked about her past."

The women's league was winding down for the night. A few bowlers were closing out their final frames. Most of the ladies had packed up their balls and shoes and were heading to the front counter to turn in their score sheets for the staff to tally up the league standings for the week. The staff had turned off the power on the empty lanes, leaving the pins standing in darkness. A kind of hush descended on the alley.

Noelle said, "Excuse me, Marlo, it's almost closing time. Let me finish my game."

She knocked off the tenth frame with a spare and a final ball to end the game. Not a bad score, considering she hadn't bowled in years. Noelle stuffed the score sheet into her bag and packed her shoes and ball as the overhead lights began shutting off and the league members filed out the building.

"Come with me," Noelle said. "We'll talk outside."

Marlo left her ball on the ball return and returned her barely used rental shoes at the counter. The women went outside and stood beside the Bug. Noelle suggested they go to The Igloo, the town's drug store and soda shop, and continue talking.

"No, I have to go," said Marlo. "I don't want anyone from SPARK to see me. And I don't want to get you into trouble. You're the only person I've told this to."

"I appreciate that. What about you? Are you safe?"

"I think so, as long as First Sage doesn't go back to Riverbend. Do you think you can help me?"

"I'll try. I'll do everything I can to find out about Blossom. I mean, Janet. You can count on that."

"Thanks." Marlo ran across the parking lot without a goodbye.

Noelle called after her, but Marlo jumped in a dirty old sedan and drove off. Noelle got into her car, but following Marlo seemed pointless. The girl had apparently told her everything she knew or wanted to say about Janet and SPARK. Driving after Marlo might spook the girl, who seemed frightened already.

Back home at the cottage, Noelle let Ceebee in the house, fed him, and then changed into her PJs. What a tiring day. Marlo's story helped to make sense of why Blossom was upset. Who was the man who had struck Blossom? First Sage—or someone else?

Noelle had only grabbed a quick sandwich to eat before she'd headed to the lanes, so now she opened a can of Campbell's chicken noodle soup to heat on the stove. Chicken soup reminded her of the mystery man in the camper—who was he? Why hadn't he left the vehicle to attend the rally? Noelle's brain hurt trying to piece it all together. She picked up the day's edition of the *Herald* but she was too tired to read anything except the funnies. Tomorrow she'd have to touch base with Trevor and find out what happened to his missing story. Or maybe there was more to his story than he could print.

Too tired to think, Noelle put The Mamas and The Papas' debut album, *If You Can Believe Your Eyes and Ears,* on the hi-fi turntable and hit "play." The gentle, four-part harmonies helped take her mind off bodies and cults. She let the music drone away in the background while she sprawled across the sofa and relaxed with a pencil and a book of crossword puzzles, getting up once to flip the disc over. She'd hit the sack right after her cousin's weather report on the ten o'clock news. At seventeen minutes after the hour, Mamie Sprinkle appeared in her trademark ponytail and enthusiasm. Using colored markers, she quickly covered her plastic wall map of the USA with numbers and symbols depicting the nation's temperatures, high, lows and rain. As Noelle watched, something jiggled in her brain.

She sat up, grabbed the Princess phone, and called Hanover. She told him she knew a way SIAMESE could bait Old Scratch out of hiding.

Chapter 13: Your Auntie Grizelda
Friday

In the Friday morning *Herald*, the True Believers Congregation ran a full-page color advertisement that was a tirade against SPARK, along with ominous warnings for anyone who dared to lead anyone astray from the one true path of salvation. When Noelle read the paper, the rant came as a jolt, as the local ragsheet generally steered clear of controversial topics and divisive politics, even during election season.

What she didn't see in the paper was a story by Trevor about SPARK—only a black-and-white ad for a free public rally to hear Wise One on Sunday in Poinsettia Park. Noelle decided to drop by the *Herald* office, not only to give the publisher a piece of her mind about the True Believers ad, but to ask Trevor about his missing story on Blossom's death. The *Herald* office wouldn't open until ten a.m., so Noelle called her mother to see if she could visit. Between her jobs and spy work, family had taken a back seat.

Mom was indeed home, having been up since 5:30 to get the twins off to school and Dad to work, but she was still willing to cook a late breakfast for Noelle. What a mother—she still wanted to wait hand and foot on her kid. Noelle skipped breakfast and put on a pullover sweater, capris and sneakers—a visit to Mom didn't warrant fancy clothes. She let the cat outside and drove to the McNabb house on Reindeer Road. When Noelle walked in the front door, Mom had bacon and fried eggs sizzling in a cast-iron skillet. Mom, who wore stockings around the house, even when dressed in a housecoat, cut up a banana and poured a glass of orange juice for her daughter.

"Mom, you don't have to go to all this trouble," said Noelle. "I'm not that hungry."

"Adults need a good breakfast. Something more substantial than a Pop-Tart."

How did Mom know her usual breakfast fare? But she relented and let Mom baby her. Soon they were both seated at the dining table. Noelle tucked into the food while Mom cradled a cup of coffee in her hands. After some chitchat, Noelle dropped a question that had been nagging her ever since her first mission with SIAMESE when Destiny had told her about a certain black sheep among the McNabb clan.

"Mom, remembered when I called and asked you about Aunt Grizelda?" The mother eyed her daughter. "You said you couldn't tell me over the phone. So now we're not on the phone. Who is she?"

"Why are you so curious? You have plenty of other aunts and uncles who dote over you."

"What's the mystery? Do I have some rotten apples hanging from the family tree?"

Mom sighed. "I suppose you should know sometime. But don't tell your brother or sister just yet. They'd blab the story all over the playground."

"Promise."

Mom's eyes took on a far-away look. "My sister Cynthia was the wild one in the family. She wasn't a bad person, just defiant and strong willed. She wanted to live in a big city. She felt the family stifled her too much. She thought Yuletide was stuffy and dull." Noelle could relate to the feeling.

"After high school we figured she'd move to Indy, but instead she hitchhiked across the country to California. She wanted to get as far away from us as possible. I didn't hear from her much. Cynthia wrote and said she worked as a movie extra. I never found out if that were true or if she wanted to sound important. She married a man who said he was a film producer. Cynthia was vague about him too. I think the guy was up to some shady business. They divorced, but instead of coming home, my sister stayed out west. I sent her some letters and Christmas cards, but after a while I never heard back, so I stopped writing. The last time I called her phone number, it was disconnected."

"Did she have any children?"

"If she did, I never heard about them. Cynthia was closer to your Aunt Mabel than me. A few years ago, your aunt told me that Cynthia had married someone with the last name of Grizelda. But Cynthia stopped writing to Mabel too. She didn't seem to want anything more to do with us."

"I thought we had a tight-knit family."

"We do, among the relatives who are still talking to each other."

"Did anyone in the family do something to make her mad?"

"If we did, I don't know about it. Then again, your Aunt Cynthia was rather thin-skinned."

"Was Aunt Cynthia a bad person?"

"No, not really. All my sisters were close growing up. We played together and helped each other with homework. We used to plan our weddings and promised to be best maids for each other." Mom took a long sip of coffee, set the cup on the table, and stared into the liquid. "I don't know what happened to all of that. I thought I knew my sisters pretty well, but turns out I didn't. Sometimes people change over the years. When someone close doesn't reach out to you, it hurts. It's like they're keeping secrets."

Such as hiding the fact that her son is a spy. "Would you like to see Aunt Cynthia again?"

"Of course, I would. After all, she's family. But still—I don't know. She might not be the same sister I knew long ago. I'm not sure we have much in common today. Cynthia's been gone for so long my sisters and I have made our own lives without her. I don't know how she'd fit in."

"Have you thought about hiring a private investigator to track her down?"

Mom gave Noelle an odd look. Her words were harsh. "If somebody wants privacy, I respect that. I don't want to intrude where I'm not wanted." She pushed back her chair and rose to her feet. "Would you like something else to eat?"

Noelle had polished off her food. She leaned back in her chair and wiped her lips with a paper napkin. "Gosh, no, I'm stuffed to the gills. Thanks, Mom. Can I have some coffee, please?"

"Of course."

Mom picked up a cup from the sideboard and poured from the coffee pot sitting on the table. As Noelle drank, she wondered if she should share *her* secret, that a certain senior control operative of a renegade spy group was her cousin.

"Penny for your thoughts," said Mom.

Noelle glanced at her, startled. "What?"

"You look preoccupied."

"Oh, yeah, sorry. Mom, would you mind if I tried to find Aunt Cynthia?"

"I suppose not, although I don't know why you'd want to."

"You know I want to move to California. If she's still out there, maybe she could help me get settled."

"If Cynthia's in any kind of trouble, I don't want you around her."

"I'm sure she's all right. We McNabbs are pretty sensible people."

"How could you even start to look for her?"

Noelle could ask Aunt Cynthia's son. "I better run now. Thanks for the grub and the talk, Mom." She gave her mother a quick kiss. "I promise not to tell anyone about our chat."

As Noelle drove to the *Herald* office, she wondered if dredging up a family secret had been a good idea. Mom looked hurt at the memories. But if Noelle brought the prodigal back into the family, would that please Mom? Or not?

The *Herald* office was housed in a small building on Kringle Avenue. Beyond the tiny lobby was a huge open space with several desks, including Trevor's, for the reporters and copy editors. The offices for the publisher and section editors lined the walls. The air was alive with the sound of clacking typewriters, shoes thumping across the wood floor, and people talking across their desks. A faint smell of printer's ink and old pulp paper hung in the air. The darkroom and the press were buried in the basement.

Noelle found Trevor at his desk, typing. "Another hard-hitting story?"

He didn't look up. The scowl on his face and the rapid pounding of his fingers on the keys reflected his mood. "Tomorrow's big scoop. The high school's finally replacing the antiquated equipment in the science lab. Maybe they'll get maps that show the earth is round and not flat."

"Did you see the True Believers advertisement in today's paper?" Noelle asked.

"Oh, that." The reporter stopped writing and looked at her. "From what I hear, our poor receptionist has been besieged with angry phone calls about that ad. Not from SPARK, but readers who found the language too inflammatory for our saccharine sweet paper."

"Good!" said Noelle. "It's about time people woke up and paid attention."

"The ad's going to backfire on the church. People might turn against them and think more highly of SPARK."

"Why did the paper run such a nasty thing in the first place?"

Trevor rubbed his thumb and forefingers together. "Filthy lucre. Yuletide doesn't have big business that can afford expensive ads. We need all the money we can get to keep the presses rolling."

"I didn't see your story on Blossom in yesterday's paper."

"And you never will. It got pulled." He glanced at the publisher's office across the room. The door was open. He whispered, "The Old Man can hear us. Come with me"

Trevor led Noelle to the sparse break room at the back end of the building. The small room held little more than a countertop with coffee pot and a tray of stale doughnuts, a fridge for sack lunches, a sink, a small table and chairs. He took two ceramic mugs out of a wall cabinet and poured a cup of coffee for each of them. Trevor shut the door and they took seats at the table.

"Yesterday I was at my desk, writing the story," he said. "A guy struts in with an expensive suit, fedora, Italian shoes and smug look. Every cliché in the book."

"Did you see his face?"

"No. I glanced up just as the goon went into the publisher's office and closed the door. About an hour later, I went downstairs to our poor excuse of a morgue to do some research. The editor showed up and told me not to bother with any more stories about SPARK. I was told, quote, 'our readers don't find that interesting.' My great aunt's fanny. People don't hold emergency town meetings unless they're interested. I asked him, "What about the girl who died? He said, 'We'll let the police handle that.' I can kiss that Pulitzer goodbye. Then he sent me out on a cock-and-bull story about the science labs just to get me out of his hair."

"Did you ask him about the stranger?"

"Yeah, but he didn't know who he was. After the goon left, the Old Man told my editor to kill all stories about SPARK. No reason given."

"What happened? Did the guy threaten to close the paper if you ran the story? Physical violence? Beatings? Arson?"

"Now you're being melodramatic."

"Trevor, don't ask me how I know 'cause I can't tell you, but I think someone in SPARK sent the guy to kill the story on Blossom."

"You mean First Sage."

"I don't know. Maybe. If you did some more digging—"

"Sorry, Noelle. I can't print the story. What's the point?"

"Don't you want to catch Blossom's killer?"

"Sure, but I can't waste my time on a dead horse. I have other assignments to cover."

"I wish you wouldn't give up so easily. Where's that reporter can-do spirit?"

"You're thinking of the post office. They're the ones who always come through, rain or snow."

Someone knocked on the door. "Hey, what's going on in there?"

Trevor called, "Door's open."

A young woman in a skirt, blouse and matching sweater opened the door. She was holding an empty coffee mug. "You shouldn't shut the door of the break room, especially when people need coffee."

"Sorry. We're through here, anyway." He introduced Noelle to the proofreader, who just gave a quick hi, refilled her mug and left, leaving the door wide open.

Trevor picked up Noelle's mug and placed it in the sink for washing. "I better get back to the exciting world of Bunsen burners and test tubes." He refilled his cup and took it with him. They strolled out of the break room.

"You know," said Noelle as they walked, "the newspaper isn't the only form of communication. There must be a way we can get Blossom's story out to the public."

"We could try carrier pigeons. Or tacking fliers on the telephone poles. Or mailing a postcard to all the subscribers." Trevor set his coffee mug on the desk and faced his friend. "Speaking not as an objective reporter but as a friend, Noelle, be careful where you put your heart. If it turns out that SPARK is really a front for something evil, you could get hurt if you keep rooting for wrong side."

Chapter 14: With A Little Help From My Friends

Noelle returned home just minutes before Destiny arrived in a black sedan—ordinary looking on the outside but stuffed full of SIAMESE gadgets. Destiny was dressed to impress in a long-sleeved red miniskirt, black pantyhose, black plastic knee boots and large gold hoop earrings. Somehow Destiny looked fantastic in anything she wore. Noelle felt a little scruffy in comparison, so she threw on a long-sleeved miniskirt with pale purple and gold stripes. A matching square handbag, white tights and white pumps completed the outfit.

On their way to Riverbend, Noelle related her visit with Trevor. "So, Destiny, was the goon going to blow up the newspaper office if they ran the story?"

"Say what?" The veteran spy shook her head. "Strong arm tactics like that went out with Al Capone. The carrot works better than the stick, and less likely to bring out the cops. The guy probably bribed the publisher with a wad of cash."

"How do you know so much about journalism?"

Destiny smiled. "We've had some run-ins with young eager beaver reporters nipping at our heels. They're trying to expose SIAMESE for a big scoop."

Noelle was aghast. "You mean you've—"

"We kill stories, not reporters. SIAMESE feeds the newshounds false information, just enough to throw them off the scent. If your pal Trevor gets too nosey, we'll shoot him down a dead end. Don't worry. We're not behind any government cover-ups. The feds do that well enough on their own."

Noelle said nothing, but she doubted the accuracy of her partner's last statement.

They soon reached the outskirts of Riverbend and drove up a hill. At the top they reached the WOWS-TV headquarters, the only structure atop the hill, save for the transmitter tower and the parking lot. Inside the lobby, Noelle asked the receptionist if she could see Mamie Sprinkle. Usually only employees were allowed past the lobby, but Noelle had been to the studio on several occasions, and the staff knew her as the weather girl's cousin. Mamie worked past eleven o'clock at night, so she generally didn't show up the next day until afternoon.

But the spies only suffered a brief wait in the lobby before Mamie came bursting through the front door with her customary enthusiasm. The newscaster, as usual, was casually clad in black sweatshirt and sweatpants, with her hair tied back in its trademark ponytail; later on, right before airtime, she'd put on a nice pantsuit. After a brief hello, Noelle asked Mamie if she and her "friend" could speak with her in private. The weather forecaster didn't have an office as such, just a desk where she kept a phone and paperwork, along with a locker for her on-air clothes. But the company conference room was available, so Mamie and Noelle seated themselves in the padded chairs around the large oval table. Various broadcasting awards, including some for the forecaster, lined the walls. The cousins made small talk while Destiny shut the door and sat across the table from the two women.

Destiny pulled a SIAMESE ID badge from her purse and showed it to Mamie. "I'm with a secret government intelligence agency. What we say in here is confidential and doesn't leave the room. Can I count on that?"

"Absolutely." Mamie glanced at her cousin. "You have some mighty unusual friends."

Noelle shrugged. "They found me, not vice versa."

Destiny continued. "We're tracking an enemy agent who's working in the area. He's a danger to the security of the U.S.A. Will you help us?"

Mamie nodded. "Sure, I'm a true blue American. Anything to help the country, I always say. But I don't see what I can do. I'm just a weather girl in a mid-size, Midwest market."

Destiny ignored the false modesty. "We believe the enemy is buying and selling secrets related to the space race. We want to set a trap to bring him out in the open. We want your station to run a story about a new missile device being developed at the Werner TecLab in Yuletide."

Mamie laughed. "Why would the government advertise something like that? Wouldn't you want to keep it under wraps?"

"The plan was my idea," said Noelle. "Everyone knows that TecLab works on classified material."

"Yeah, but classified means they keep it hush-hush," said Mamie. "They don't brag about it on tri-state television."

"It's a false story," said Destiny. "There's no missile. But it's the type of thing that would attract the enemy's interest."

Mamie scrunched her mouth to express her skepticism. "Uh huh. But the people working at TecLab, they'd know the story was as fake as the weather forecasts at our rival stations."

"Not really," said Noelle. "Dad told me the projects are split up among the departments. For security reasons, the employees only have a piece of the puzzle, so the workers don't see the whole picture. Only the top management knows what's what, and they wouldn't confirm or deny anything."

"And if the higher-ups complain," said Destiny, "the station can say they received some misleading information from a usually reliable source."

"I don't know." Mamie crossed her arms. "Here at WOWS, we pride ourselves on accuracy. Real news you can trust. That's our motto."

"We can make it worth your while," said Destiny. "My agency is willing to pay for whatever you need. We'll cover expenses and throw in a bonus."

Mamie rested her arms on the table and leaned forward toward Destiny. "Let me get this straight. You want the anchorman to read a false story about a make-believe missile?"

"That's right," Destiny replied. "And if your studio could whip up some graphics of a cool-looking warhead and stock photos of the plant, so much the better."

Mamie frowned. "We could lose our broadcasting license over a scam like that."

"It's for the common good."

"You're saying the end justifies the means?" said Mamie.

"If you want to talk about truth, what about the advertisements your station runs?"

Mamie slumped in her chair. "I'd love to help, really, I would, but I'm not the one in charge of the news department. Slipping phony stories onto the teleprompter is not in my job description. You'd need to speak with the news director. Maybe the station manager too."

"This is getting complicated," said Noelle. "We'd have to recruit everyone at the station."

"And that's bad for business," said Destiny. "The more who know, the more leaks out."

"What makes you think this bad guy is going to see the phony broadcast anyway?" Mamie asked.

"Spies keep up with the news," said Destiny. "And your station has the biggest ratings."

"I appreciate the flattery," said Mamie, "but no can do."

"Wait a sec," said Noelle. "Mamie, what if you talk about it in your forecast? A little aside like, 'The predicted rain won't stop the new defense missile from landing at the plant?' Corny, but it might work."

"Say, cousin, that isn't a bad idea," said Mamie.

"It's a bit subtle," Destiny mused.

"Subtle is good," said the weather girl. "If you're trying to fool someone, won't do to toot your horn too loudly."

Noelle got excited. "Of course, it'll work. Mamie gets silly all the time on her broadcasts. Most viewers just laugh at her."

"Thanks a lot, coz." She didn't sound appreciative.

"I meant it in a good way. The regular watchers will think it's just part of the act. The enemy is the only one who'll take it seriously."

Destiny thought for a moment. "What if he turns off the news before the weather report?"

"This is Indiana," said Mamie. "Everybody watches the weather report."

Noelle asked, "Mamie, will you get in trouble with your boss over a fake forecast?"

"Most of the time he doesn't pay attention to me. As long as the ratings stay up, he pretty much lets me do as I please."

"All right," said Destiny. "How soon can you swing it?"

"Today, if you want."

"Perfect. Remember, keep this on the low down. Better set up a cover story in case your boss catches on."

"Will do."

Destiny stood up, reached across the table, and shook Mamie's hand. "Thank you. You never saw us or had this conversation."

Mamie passed her palm in front of her face. "Whoosh! Wiped it right out of my mind."

Noelle got on her feet as well. "Bye, Mamie. Thanks again for helping us."

"My pleasure. Say, coz, when are you coming over for a visit? Haven't seen you in coon's ages."

"I've been busy."

"With this spy stuff?"

Noelle grinned. "Maybe."

* * * * *

Friday night meant Noelle was back at work at the Cozy Christmas Family Fun Park, playing the role of the Winter Witch in several evening performances of a silly musical sketch called The Candy Cane Capers. Over the weekend, she'd have to juggle her sleuthing and spy work around her acting job. On Fridays the cast and crew had an early call for a pick-up rehearsal to refresh everyone after the weeklong hiatus. After Destiny dropped off Noelle at the cottage, the actress barely had time to gobble a PB&J sandwich and feed the ever-hungry Ceebee before she rushed out the door. She didn't bother to change clothes, as she'd be in her witch costume and green makeup all evening.

But before Noelle could entertain the tourists at the theme park, she had to first stop at the police station, where she stood in line at the front counter— in Yuletide, "a line" meant waiting behind more than one person. Someone had to pay a ticket for an expired parking meter, and another resident filed a complaint about a barking dog. Such were the "crimes" of Yuletide. Noelle asked the desk clerk if she could speak with Chief Whitlock. The clerk took her to the chief's office, a small, cramped room as unappealing as its occupant. The white walls were decorated with bulletin boards pinned with wanted posters and pages of new state laws. Whitlock's framed associate of science degree from Vincennes University was hung on a wall.

As usual, the chief was sprawled in the armchair at his desk, his bulk spreading over the seat and his hands folded over his considerable gut. As usual, he was not pleased to see her. "Hello, missy. I guess you're here to get on my case about the dead hippie."

"I wouldn't put it that way but, yes, I'd like to know what you've found out about Blossom."

As Noelle stood in front of the chief's desk, something caught her eye. She crossed the room to inspect it. A small shelf on the wall held a trophy with a wooden base and a marble column holding a gold-painted image of a football player.

"What's this?"

Whitlock sat straight in his chair and beamed. "That's my Most Valuable Player Award from the year Yuletide High won the regional football tournament. That photo on the wall beside it? That's the championship Elves team."

"Oh! I see you! Is that you in the back row on the left?" She felt it best not to mention that Whitlock looked far leaner and trimmer in the picture than he did today.

"Yup, that's me. My senior year. I was the star quarterback. I made the winning touchdown in the last five seconds of the game. I won that puppy for the school."

"You must be very proud. Say, wasn't that the only year the school won regional in football?"

"Yeah, after that victory the Elves just never got it together again." He sounded hurt, as if somehow the losses were his fault.

"Did you play football in college?"

Whitlock slumped in the chair and his face lost its glow. "Yeah, a little. I wanted to grab a football scholarship for Purdue or IU. But the coach at VU didn't like me. Kept me benched most of the time, so I called it quits on a four-year school and joined the force instead." His voice resumed its usual lethargy. "So, have a seat." He gestured at the empty chair in front of the desk.

"Thanks." The seat sagged a little when Noelle put her weight on it. The furniture in the room seemed as old as the town itself. "Anything new on Blossom's death?"

"You know, that case is the craziest thing I've ever seen."

"Why so?"

Whitlock leaned forward; the chair springs creaked. He rested his forearms on the desk. "Remember the syringe we found beside the body? I sent it off to the lab in Indy for testing. Know what we found?"

Noel held her breath in expectation. "What?"

He grinned, relishing the irony. "Zip. Nada. Not a trace of nothin'."

Her hopes fell faster than a plunging elevator. "No drugs?"

"Clean as a whistle. The needle was spotless too. No fingerprints. The darn thing hadn't ever been used."

"That proves Blossom didn't touch the syringe. A junkie doesn't wipe off his fingerprints. So how did Blossom die?"

"You got me, kiddo. Maybe a snake bit her."

Noelle crossed her arms and sulked. Her theory about murder was washing away like the spring rain. Maybe the death was indeed due to natural causes. Maybe Blossom had a hidden health condition. But yet—

"But if the syringe hadn't been used," she said, "What was it doing there in the first place?"

"Maybe a camper dropped it last summer. You can find all kinds of junk at that place."

"Chief, do you have the photographs of the body?"

"Well, sure."

"Can I please see them?"

"You're one persistent girl. Why don't you take up a nice hobby like knitting instead of playing Nancy Drew?"

Noelle glared in response. When she refused to leave, Whitlock lumbered to his feet, opened a squeaky drawer of the filing cabinet, and removed a manila folder. He resumed his seat and spread out the file's various papers and photos across his desk. Noelle examined the photos until she found one that showed the body, spread on the ground with the head tilted to one side. She held the picture beneath the desk lamp for extra light. She asked the chief for a magnifying glass and, to her amazement, he actually had one, tucked away in another file drawer. Noelle took a tissue out of her purse, wiped the dusty lens, and held the glass over the photo.

"Chief, look here." She handed the lens and picture to him. "There's a big bruise on the back of Blossom's head. It's hard to see with her long hair, but it's there. See that dark spot?"

He looked through the lens. "Maybe it's a shadow."

"No, we were at the campgrounds about midday. The sun would have been straight overhead. No shadows."

"So you're thinking someone clunked her on the head?"

"And look, there's bruising on her face."

"Maybe she tripped and fell and cracked her skull on one of the benches."

Noelle struggled to hold her tongue. How could the local school system, one of the best for a small rural town, produce someone so obtuse?

"Her sleeve is torn in a couple of places. She was in a fight with someone."

"Looks that way, don't it?"

"I think you should order an autopsy right away. If Blossom didn't have any drugs in her body, then it was murder."

"Hold your horses. I got these photos, but I ain't got the corpse. Not enough room in the station fridge." She didn't laugh at the joke. "The funeral home took the body. Let me give them a ring."

As the chief sat and dialed the black rotary phone on his desk, Noelle looked over the other photos and reports. What seemed like a simple case was getting more complicated than she had imagined. After a brief chat with the local mortician, Whitlock hung up the phone.

"Well?" Noelle tapped her foot on the floor, eager to get a move on it.

"The director said he'd be happy to help us."

"Yes?" She brightened.

"But he can't. Yesterday they cremated the body."

Chapter 15: The River Is Wide

Could this case get any weirder? "Cremated?" she echoed.

"The girl's family wanted a regular burial. The cult wanted cremation 'cause they got a weird idea that destroying the body frees the soul," explained Whitlock. "The family's gonna bury the ashes in the family plot in Illinois."

Noelle was too stunned to think any further. "I guess that takes care of that."

"That don't mean the investigation is closed," he lied. "I'll let you know if anything else turns up."

"You're just going to leave it at that?"

"What can I do without a body? If we're lucky and someone shows up and confesses, then we got a case."

Noelle murmured a brief goodbye and left, mulling over the case as she drove to the theme park. The needle was no accident. In the fall, after the summer tourists had left, the Holiday Acres cleanup crew always did a thorough job of picking up the seasonal trash. They would certainly see something as large as a syringe and would not leave it for a kid to pick up. Noelle had a nagging feeling that she'd missed something when she was at the campgrounds on Wednesday. Two days had passed, but the devotees would not want to return to the scene of the crime, so any evidence might still be in place.

As Noelle pulled into the employees' parking lot at the theme park, she started making plans for tomorrow. She'd return to the fire pit and search for clues—but first, she had the show to do. Acting in the goofy Christmas romp kept her mind off spies and murderers for a while. Between shows, she called Trevor from the pay phone outside the dressing rooms and asked if he was free tomorrow. The reporter didn't work Saturdays, since nothing happened in Yuletide over weekends except the local school games that the sports writer covered. Trevor agreed to return to Holiday Acres with her and poke around. After Noelle's performances ended, she headed home to relax with a cold Frostie root beer and the ten o'clock news. She was anxious to see if Mamie would carry out their plan.

Mamie frequently dressed up and did goofy things for her broadcasts, part of her appeal to the viewers. Tonight, she showed up in front of the camera wearing a low-brim hat and a buttoned trench coat with the collar pulled up around her neck.

"Attention, all spies," Mamie began.

Noelle nearly fell off the sofa. Nothing like being obvious.

"Today's secret code word is *rain*," said the weather girl. "Yep, bundle up in your trench coats 'cause it's gonna pour tomorrow, babies. It'll be raining so hard you'd think Russia was dropping bombs on us. But don't fret. The Werner TecLab plant in Yuletide just got in a bunch of plans for a brand-new nuclear missile guaranteed to blow the Reds right out of Asia. You can't beat good old American know-how, especially in our own backyard."

Mamie removed her hat and switched gears to give a serious description of the nation's weather for the next day. But Noelle barely heard her. Would Old Scratch take the jest seriously? Was the enemy agent watching? Would Noelle really need her raincoat tomorrow?

* * * * *

Saturday

The next morning Mamie's forecast came true—rain was pouring down, light but steady. Noelle put on clothes suitable for walking around in the rain—pants, turtleneck sweater and black leather "Beatle boots"— and was on her way out the door when the phone rang. She picked it up, assuming it was a message from SIAMESE. She guessed wrong.

"Hey, Noelle, it's Julia."

Dealing with wedding plans was the last thing Noelle wanted to do right now. But she put on a pleasant voice. "Hi, Julia. What's up?"

"I've been trying to call you all week, but you're never home. I can't get you at the record store either. What have you been doing?"

"This and that. Lots going on."

"Well, okay. Just want to let you know that today my bridesmaids and I are all going shopping for dresses. We want to check out some bridal shops in Riverbend. It'll be more fun if we do it all together. I need you to come along."

Noelle covered the phone mouthpiece and let out a soft groan before she replied. "I'm sorry, Julia, but I already made other plans."

"Well, reschedule. What's more important than shopping for wedding dresses?"

Noelle was dying to say 'solving a murder case,' but Julia wouldn't understand. "This is pretty short notice. I can't postpone my appointment."

"Oh, come on, Noelle. There's nothing to do in this town on a Saturday, and I know you don't work at the park until this evening. We'll be back in plenty of time."

Truth be told, Noelle loved shopping for clothes—by herself. But having hit the boutiques with Julia in the past, she knew the shopping trek would be a long, tiring ordeal, with the bride-to-be trying on every dress in the store, disliking every one, and taking forever to make up her mind. Besides, Noelle needed to get to the campgrounds before the rain washed away the clues.

"Tell you what, Julia, you gals pick out the dress, give me the name of the store and the item number, and I'll go in when I can and order it myself."

"I had my heart set on buying everything today. I've heard of brides who order their dresses too late, and they don't arrive in time for the ceremony."

"I'll get my dress right away. I promise."

Julia let out an exasperated sigh. "Noelle, don't be such a wimp. We're going to make it fun, have lunch together and all that. Besides, some stores give discounts if you buy all your dresses at the same time."

"Look, I'll give you my measurements so you can order for me. I don't need to be there to try things on." As an actress who had worked with costumers, Noelle knew her dress size.

"If I didn't know better, Noelle, I'd think you didn't want to do this. I want all my girls together, you know, so we can make this a big celebration together."

"I'm sorry, Julia. I don't mean to throw a wet blanket on your big day. I know this is special for you. But could you do this next weekend? Or you and I can shop together some other time, just the two of us? I really can't get out of my appointment."

From the tone of Julia's voice, Noelle could picture her pouting. "All right. I guess if you can't come today, you can't. Now, will you be able to make the rehearsal dinner and the wedding? Or will you be busy then?"

"I can make it. I'll clear my calendar and mark the day in red. Grab a pencil and I'll give you my measurements." Noelle hastily quoted the figures. "Thanks, Julia. By the way, what are your colors?"

"Lavender for both my maid and matron of honor. Yellow for the flower girl, and pink for the bridesmaids. Won't that be pretty?"

Noelle groaned again. With her dark hair and skin tone, she looked terrible in pink. "That sounds nice. I have to run. Bye, now. Happy shopping."

The rain was falling when Noelle finally arrived at the campgrounds. Trevor was sitting in his GTO, drumming his fingers on the steering wheel. She pulled the Bug beside his car and got out. He rolled down the coupe's driver's side window so they could talk.

She put her hands on the window ledge. "I'm sorry I'm late. Julia called me and you know how she gabs."

"Julia? What did she want?"

"I'm one of her bridesmaids, and she's going shopping for the dresses in the pouring rain. Believe me, tromping around here in the mud will be more fun that window-shopping with Julia."

"I'm glad you made it. I was ready to leave."

"So, let's go."

The reporter kept the rain at bay with a brown raincoat and an open umbrella. Noelle shivered in her plastic slicker and plastic rain bonnet; at least the slacks kept her legs warm. She'd left her umbrella at home because it would get in the way. They stopped at the office to check in with Mr. Woodman, who assured them that no trespassers had been on the grounds since Wednesday. Thursday morning he'd hired additional security guards to patrol the area, day and night. Noelle wanted to speak with First Sage, but the manager said the devotees were away "witnessing" at the other small towns surrounding Yuletide. In the past two days, Mr.

Woodman said, the group had not left the cabin area except for yesterday's rally in Riverbend. Nobody had returned to the fire pit, which is where Noelle and Trevor headed.

The rain eased up. The downpour had dampened the ground, but not enough to wash away any objects. Noelle and Trevor separated, each one examining different areas around the stone fire pit. At the end of their search, they had found some loose buttons, broken shoelaces, scraps of paper and bits of leather left over from a summer crafts project, all from months ago. They tossed the trash into the nearby waste bin.

"I think we're at the end of the trail, Noelle." Trevor put his hands on his hips. "If Blossom was killed, I don't see how you're going to prove it."

"Something has to turn up. It just has to." Noelle squatted by the place where the body had lain. She peered carefully at the ground, and then squealed in delight. "Trevor, come here, look at this!" He leaned over, and she pointed at a rock. "See this dark mark? This has to be dried blood!"

"Looks like a water stain to me."

"No, it's blood."

"Are you sure?"

"Sure, I'm sure. When I was in fifth grade, a kid fell off the jungle gym at school. He hit his head on the concrete playground and left this same kind of mark. I remember it clearly."

"Too bad we can't test the blood. If we still had the body, we could see if it matches Blossom's blood type."

She straightened up. "Nobody else has been in this area since summer. Any blood stains from last year would have worn away by now."

"But it doesn't prove whether Blossom fell by accident or was pushed. And if she was murdered, how did the killer get on the grounds? Everyone has to park in the front lot, and Mr. Woodman can see the cars from the office window. It's too far to walk from town to the camp. At sunset the gate is locked."

"Why do you love to shoot holes in my theories?"

Trevor took her chin in his hand. "Because I don't want you running off half-cocked in the wrong direction and hurting yourself."

Trevor sat down on a bench. Noelle poked around some more. "Hey! Something's wedged against the leg of this bench. I missed it before."

"What is it?"

"I'm not sure." She stooped over and pulled out a dirty strip of paper. "Looks like a bus ticket. Maybe the killer came here from out of town."

"Where's it from?"

"Hard to tell. The ink's smudged." Noelle put the ticket in her purse. "It's too cloudy here. I'll have to look it over at home under a lamp."

She sat beside Trevor and gazed out over the lake. The drizzle formed dimples in the water. The air smelled fresh from the cleansing rain. The birds in the trees began their noisy chatter.

"It's so pretty here," she said. "Serene, peaceful. The water seems to go on forever. What a shame to spoil it with such—" She stopped talking.

"Noelle? What's wrong?"

She continued to stare at the rippling water. "That's it! It has to be it! Look!" Noelle grabbed his arm with one hand, and pointed over the water with the other. "We've been looking at this all wrong. The killer didn't arrive in a car. He came by boat!"

"Is that possible? I thought the lake was inside the camp."

"No, it goes on for several miles. When I was a kid at summer camp, I tried walking all the way around the lake but I couldn't; it's too far by foot. The camp ends a little way down that way and then it becomes private property owned by someone else. There's a fence on the ground to mark the end of the property, but there's no barrier across the lake. Anyone could grab a boat or raft and make their way into the campgrounds."

"That sounds reasonable. Let's check it out."

They returned to the parking lot to retrieve Trevor's car. They drove along one of the service roads that ran through the grounds until they reached the metal link fence that marked the boundary. The rain had stopped, and the sun began peeking through the clouds. Trevor left his umbrella in the car as they got out. They climbed over the low fence, and found a gravel road that followed the shoreline. After a brisk walk, they reached a wooden dock, a shack and a genteel old man sitting in a plastic lawn chair. A large lawn umbrella set up behind the chair sheltered him from the weather. He wore denim pants, heavy boots and a thick jacket over a pullover sweater.

"Howdy, folks," he called. "Name's Clement. Kinda soggy day to be out walking about. What can I do fer you?"

Trevor indicated the shed. "Do you live here?"

"Gosh, no, I got a nice house in town. This here's my business. I rent boats. Folks can go fishin' or just take a scenic trip down the lake." The man waggled his white eyebrows. "Lots of couples go out sparkin' on the water."

Noelle glanced at Trevor and then rolled her eyes. The man thought they were a romantic item!

But Trevor continued undaunted. "You rent boats? How much?"

154 Hippie Haven Homicide

Clement rattled off the prices, based on length of time on the water, size of the boat and number of passengers.

"Sounds like fun," said Noelle. "The lake is beautiful. I bet you keep busy."

"I do in the summer. People like to come here in the heat and cool down. Lots of folks go fishin' too. You gotta bring your own equipment for that. Right now, it's my slow time of the year. Too cold and wet for the locals to be out here. But sometimes the tourists drop by, the ones who just gotta see every blessed thing in town."

"Have you had any customers this week?" asked Trevor.

"A few."

"Do people row over to the campgrounds?" Noelle asked.

"Sure, all the time."

"What about Wednesday?" she asked. "Anyone here last Wednesday?"

"Say, what's with the questions? Are you gonna rent a boat or not?"

"Yeah, we are," said Trevor. Noelle shot him a glance. "A friend of ours may have been here earlier this week. If he enjoyed his ride, then we know we'll like it too."

"Of course, he liked it. What's not to like? The sun, the birds, the fish, the water . . ."

"What was his name?"

Clement spat some tobacco juice onto the ground. "You don't know your friend's name?"

"I mean, we had several friends who were planning a trip," said Trevor. "But we don't know who made it."

The man scratched his thigh. "I generally don't ask for names. The customers I don't know, they're from out of town, and I never see them again. Let's see,

Wednesday? That would be three days ago. Yeah, I remember now. I remember 'cause I rarely get singles. It's always couples or groups or families. I remember the hair. Red hair. Kinda like yours," he pointed at Trevor, "but more orange-y and brighter."

"You're very observant," said Trevor. "What else can you tell us about his appearance?"

Clement tilted his head and squinted at the pair. "You don't know what your friend looks like?" A car drove up on the gravel road and stopped beside the shack. "Now, do you want a boat or not? If not, I got other customers."

Trevor pulled out a wallet from his pants pocket and paid for a thirty-minute rental, the shortest and cheapest available. Clement untied one of the smaller rowboats and soon Trevor and Noelle were on the waters. The reporter rowed the craft toward Holiday Acres and halted.

"Why are you stopping?" Noelle asked.

Trevor pulled the oars out of the water and set them inside the boat. "We don't have to go all the way to the fire pit, do we? Now that we know we can get there from here. Besides, I have to row back and I'm saving my strength."

"Anyway, at least we have a description of our killer."

"Alleged killer. There's no proof this mystery man was the one who killed the girl. All we know is that the guy has red hair, which isn't much to go on. And he isn't local, or Clement would have known his name. Everyone in Yuletide knows everyone." He said this as if it were a bad thing. "Anyway, the geezer was getting too suspicious for me to keep grilling him. But Clement was right about one thing. If mister redhead came from out of town, we'll never see him again."

"He might return to make sure Blossom is dead."

"Then he can't be a professional hit man. They don't run off unless the job's done right."

"Blossom's ex-boyfriend is still a possibility. He's from out of town. I've met him."

"Does he have red hair?"

"I don't know. He had the hood of his jacket pulled up over his hair."

Trevor gazed off over the land. "Why don't we just relax and enjoy the scenery?"

"I bet this would be gorgeous at night with the stars twinkling overhead and a full moon and an owl hooting in the distance. Perfect for couples."

He raised an eyebrow at her. "I never pegged you as the romantic type."

Noelle shot him a glance. "Well, a girl can dream about Mister Right, even if she never finds him." She watched the fish gliding beneath the water until Trevor interrupted her thoughts.

"Does anyone from True Believers have red hair?" he asked.

"Trevor! You don't think a church person would commit murder!"

"The ad in the *Herald* took some mighty big pot shots at the cult."

"I can't image anyone going that far just because they dislike someone," said Noelle.

"Blacks were lynched because of their skin. That's why they're protesting for their civic rights," he said. "Do you know anyone in this True Believers clan?"

"No. I know people from the other churches in town. I've done service projects with the Catholics at Holy Nativity, but not that group. They're new in town, and so far, they haven't mingled with anyone else."

"If they're so exclusive, I'd have to ask what they're hiding."

The two were bored with drifting along the lake in the cold weather, so Trevor rowed back to the boat dock before their thirty minutes were up. Noelle picked up her car in the parking lot and soon was back home inside her cottage. She wanted to call Hanover to see if the mystery man matched anyone in the SIAMESE files, but she had no description beyond the hair color.

But sleuthing for the killer would have to wait. After performing her evening shows at the theme park, Destiny was going to pick her up to stake out Werner TecLab in hopes that Old Scratch would fall for the trap that Mamie helped to set. Noelle put her wet clothes in the wicker laundry hamper, washed the mud off her boots, and took a nap so she'd be fresh for her work at the park, followed by a night of intrigue.

Chapter 16: Come And Get It
Sunday

Just after midnight, Destiny and Noelle drove up to the Werner TecLab plant in a SIAMESE sedan. The car engine had been adapted to run silent. Destiny switched on the infrared headlights to keep the black car hidden. Both women were clad in what Noelle described as their skulking clothes: Destiny in a black jumpsuit and black low-heeled boots, and Noelle in an all-black ensemble of a long-sleeved shirt, pants, socks and sneakers.

On the drive, Noelle told Destiny about her conversation with her mother about her mysterious aunt. "Do you have any idea how I can find Aunt Grizelda?"

"No, and if I did, I wouldn't blab. We have a rule at SIAMESE: we don't talk personal. If we're caught by the enemy, we won't betray anyone 'cause we don't know who they are."

"Do your parents know what you do?"

"You're a little snoop."

"I just like to get to know people, that's all. Gosh, Destiny, sometimes you act like a robot, all data and no feelings."

"It's in my job description." She turned off Kringle Avenue and onto the street that led to the plant. "Never knew my daddy. He disappeared when I was young. My mama thinks I travel around selling cosmetics. I don't want her to know the truth 'cause she'd worry. She's raising my brothers. and she's got plenty else to fret over."

"Do you see your mama often?"

Destiny kept her eyes on the road. "I don't want the enemy following me and finding out where she lives."

"Wow. I don't know what I'd do if I couldn't see my family. Sounds like you give up a lot when you're in SIAMESE."

"There's the plant up ahead. Time to get to work."

On a small hill at the end of the road loomed the four-story Werner TecLab facility. The plant provided many well-paying blue- and white-collar jobs for the community, especially for the voc-tech graduates of Yuletide High. Noelle had attended several of the plant's public open houses, where her dad showed off his office and the labs where he worked. In the daytime. the windows were lit up for the hundreds of employees who roamed the halls. In the velvet night, however, the dark building resembled a haunted house. To bypass the guard shack at the entrance, Destiny drove off the road and onto the mowed lawn that surrounded the building. She circled around to the back of the complex. The ground had dried enough between rains to be firm, not muddy.

"Once we're inside, I can guide you around," said Noelle.

"I know the layout."

"How did you get a map of the place? Isn't that classified information?"

Destiny shot her a look. "It's our job to get information. SIAMESE has the specs on all the companies that do business with the feds." She parked the car behind a thick line of trees. The women got out of the car. "And here's your flashlight." Destiny handed Noelle a thin metal cylinder. "Much better than that old Girl Scout lantern you used to carry around."

Noelle glowered but took the gift anyway. "Thanks."

"The plant's closed on Sunday, right?" Noelle nodded. "Good. We won't be running into any early bird workers."

With the nearly full moon and the security lights atop tall poles, the women didn't need their flashlights. No rain was falling in the clear night; the women wouldn't be leaving footprints. A tall, stone wall stood between them and the backside of the plant.

"I don't see a door in the wall," said Noelle. "What do we do, jump over?"

"You got it." Destiny opened the trunk of the car and removed a large metal cylinder with long cloth straps attached to it. Two bent rods protruded from the sides of the object. "Turn around."

"What for?"

"So I can put this on you. Will you shut up and stop asking so many questions."

As much as Noelle enjoyed working the missions, she wished that the SIAMESE cats would stop treating her like a child. Destiny wrapped the black straps around Noelle's thighs and under her arms to secure the cylinder to her back. Noelle started to tip over from the weight of the cylinder. She had a feeling she wasn't going to like what was coming next.

"Comfortable?" said Destiny.

"Not really."

"You'll learn to like it."

The spy showed Noelle how to operate the two rods that stuck out from the cylinder, one on either side of her body. Pressing a button on one rod ignited the jetpack's engine. Moving the levers up would lift her, and tilting them to the side would help her turn.

"Just nudge the rods a tad. They're sensitive," said Destiny. "Go straight up and down. Don't get fancy on your first flight. Make sure you're clear of the wall before you drop. Don't turn off the jet before you land or you'll fall hard. Ease yourself down nice and slow. I don't want to have to scoop you off the ground."

"You won't. What if a guard sees me?"

"He won't. The guards are at the front gate. They're not expecting any flyovers."

Destiny pulled a second cylinder onto her own back, much like putting on a backpack. She buckled the straps and adjusted the device to fit her. She told Noelle to go first in case she couldn't make it over the wall. Noelle licked her lips and pushed the "on" button. The surprisingly quiet engine lit up. The exhaust felt hot again the back of her legs—what if her pants caught fire? She trembled from the vibrations of the motor against her back. Could she control the monster? Destiny made a "you okay?" sign with finger and thumb. Noelle nodded. The spy jerked her thumb upward, the signal for Noelle to move.

She grabbed the rods with both hands and jerked too hard. The jetpack shot up like a champagne cork, pushing Noelle into the air and leaving her stomach back on Earth. The force pushed back her head. The sudden rush stunned her, and she didn't notice that she'd cleared the wall—and then some. Noelle kept rising. She tugged on the rods and began to plummet. She quickly adjusted the controls until she was just hovering over the wall. Before descending she checked to make sure she'd be landing on the correct side of the wall and avoiding a chewing out for failing her first rocket ride. Even with her knees bent to absorb the shock, Noelle landed harder than she wanted. But at least she wasn't flat on her back. She turned off the jetpack and tried to stop swaying.

Destiny landed beside her with the agility of an angel. She too cut her engine. "Not bad for a beginner. No broken bones?" Noelle shook her head, more to clear it than to communicate. "For a minute I thought you were going to catch up with Sputnik."

"This would make a great a ride for the theme park."

Destiny helped her out of the straps and removed her own jetpack. She hid the devices beneath some shrubs; they'd need the jetpacks later for their escape back over the wall. The spies crossed a narrow strip of pavement and approached the backside of the brick TecLab building. The back door was set inside a recess with a light bulb burning above. A box welded beside the door held a security device: a keypad with a slot to insert an identification card.

"How do we get inside?" Noelle asked.

"Easy," said Destiny. "We walk in like everyone else."

"We're not going in through a window?"

"And leave behind a cut pane of glass to announce to everyone that we were here? Don't think so."

"But we need a passcode to get through this door."

"Piece of cake."

"I should have brought my dad's ID card," said Noelle.

"No good. Devices like this keep track each time a card is used. We don't want to get your old man into trouble." Destiny removed a slim metal plate from the black pouch that hung from her belt. She slipped the object into the slot. "This sets up a dummy account." The lights on the card reader flashed and the door popped opened. "The door lets in a fictitious employee." The women entered the building. The door automatically shut behind them.

"Won't someone notice the fake name?" Noelle asked.

"The data I fed in will delete itself in ten seconds. Won't leave a record behind."

They stood in a small alcove that opened into the corridor. Noelle started to move, but Destiny held out her arm to stop her. "We gotta take care of the cameras first."

"What cameras? I've never noticed cameras in here."

"They're set in those big glass circles right under the ceiling at the end of the hall."

Destiny opened her pouch and removed two metal boxes about the size of cigarette packs. She handed one to Noelle. "When I say go, step out in the hall and aim this end of the gizmo at the camera lens to your right. Press the red button and keep it down until I say stop. I'll take the camera on the left. We gotta do this together or one of those electronic eyeballs will catch what we're doing. Got it?"

Noelle nodded. Destiny gave a one-two-three countdown, and the women sprang into the hall. Now that Noelle knew what to look for, she easily spotted the camera on the east wall; she'd always thought the glass circle was just a window. She held her arms out straight and pushed the button. A narrow red beam shot out from the end of the device and bore into the glass. Destiny aimed her device at the west wall. After a few seconds she called stop and grabbed Noelle's hand. Together they ran down the hall toward the elevator doors. The main overhead lights had been turned off for the night, but small security lights glowed along the top of the walls, providing enough illumination for the guards to walk their rounds. Noelle reached out to press a button on the elevator, but Destiny hustled her into the nearby stairwell.

"Where to now?" Noelle asked.

"Top floor," said Destiny. "That's where the bigwigs hang out."

"The elevator would be quicker."

"It records the number of times it goes up and down during the day."

"How does Dad manage to work in a place like this that keeps track of every step you take?"

"He's probably used to it." Destiny zipped up the stairs like a gazelle.

Noelle followed, panting to keep up. Still, despite the effort she kept talking. "What did we just do to the cameras downstairs?"

"We confused them. Those cameras aren't sophisticated, and they're easy to fool. They just record images. They don't sense movement, heat or sound. What we did was overload the circuits to make some static and scramble the view. Anyone watching a monitor would think it was a power surge. But you can't leave it on for long or the guards get suspicious."

Noelle was out of breath when they reached the top floor; Destiny was hardly winded. She opened the stairwell door, and they stepped into another long hallway.

"Don't we have to put out the cameras here?" Noelle asked.

"No cameras. The architect figured that any intruders would enter on the ground floor."

"My dad's office is on the third floor."

"He's middle management. The important stuff is up here with the top brass."

The women turned on their flashlights and entered a dark room that, on first glance, looked like any other executive suite with desks and typewriters for the secretaries as well as doors leading to the administrators' offices. The wall opposite the door held a bank of windows covered with plastic blinds, now closed. The main difference between this and most office suites was a floor-to-ceiling safe built into one wall.

"How will Old Scratch know where to find us?" Noelle asked.

"Common sense. Nobody's gonna leave missile blueprints lying around on a desk. This is the only safe in the place. He'll assume the plans are in there. And now we wait."

The women turned off their flashlights and crouched behind a desk where they could keep an eye on both the hall door and the safe. With the room lamps off, the only illumination came from slivers of moonlight seeping between the window blinds. After a while Noelle became cramped and restless. She tried to stretch out a leg. Suppose they sat here all night for nothing? Did Old Scratch miss the broadcast, or did he know it was a joke? Did Mamie get into trouble with her station manager over the hoax? Would Noelle get home in time to feed a starving Ceebee?

Destiny finally broke the silence with a whisper. "Our pal should be here by now. He'd want to be in and out before dawn. I'll check the hall. Wait here."

Destiny slipped silently out of the room. Noelle yawned. A sharp noise, like metal scraping against concrete, roused her. The sound came from outside. She turned her head. Was someone coming through a window? Hardly seemed likely, as the building had no fire escapes to climb, and the brickwork was too smooth to provide handholds. She heard the noise again. Something was definitely going on. Noelle tiptoed to the window. She pulled down one of the blinds, just enough to peek out. A large metal hook had embedded itself in the windowsill; a rope ladder hung from the hook. Someone with an air gun had shot the hook and ladder up in the air.

And that person was quickly scrambling up the cord rungs.

Noelle sucked in her breath. Within seconds the intruder would be in the room. She ran into the hall, not caring how much noise she made.

"Destiny! Destiny!" she shouted.

Her partner was at the far end of the hall. "Keep your voice down!"

"He's here! He's climbing up a ladder!"

"Of all the sneaky—I should have thought of that. Come on!"

The women returned to the suite just as the intruder pushed up a windowpane. The company had seen no need to install burglar alarms or locks on the top floor windows. The women ducked behind a desk as the burglar reached around the blinds, found the cord, and pulled up the shades. He was a small man, adept for climbing through windows. Noelle could barely see him, covered as he was head to toe in black sneakers, pants, turtleneck, gloves and a ski mask that covered all of his head except for his eyes and mouth. He nimbly climbed through the open window and secured the blinds up for a quick getaway. He removed a black backpack and placed it on a desk. He switched on a desk lamp and removed some safecracking tools from the backpack.

Destiny sprang to her feet and snapped on the wall switch, filling the room with a blaze of light from the overhead fluorescent tubes. Noelle blinked at the sudden light. The man froze.

"Hold it right here, Old Scratch," said Destiny.

The eyes behind the mask crinkled in confusion. "You're not a cop. Who are you?" The thin, reedy voice didn't sound like that of a hard-bitten spy.

"I'm your worst nightmare." With two quick steps Destiny was in front of the guy. She grabbed his arms and he struggled to break way. "Tabby Gray! Little help here!"

Noelle rushed over and stood behind the man. She wrapped her arms around him in a tight bear hug to pin his arms to his side. For such a small guy, he was strong. Noelle had to plant her feet firmly to keep him from knocking her over. Destiny yanked off the man's ski mask. He was in his twenties, wide-eyed and terrified, not the sort of foe Noelle had expected.

"Okay, let him go," Destiny said. "He won't make a break for it."

Noelle released the man with gratitude. She couldn't have held on much longer.

Destiny eyed the man with disbelief. "You're Old Scratch?"

"Who?"

"You know who. The spy who sells military secrets."

"I don't know what you're talking about, lady. I'm just a cat burglar. A guy hired me to steal some papers he said was in this safe."

"I need the name of the guy who hired you."

"I dunno who he is. Really. I got a call from a friend of a friend. Asked if I wanted to make some quick dough. I said, sure, why not, long as nobody gets hurt."

"What are these papers you're supposed to pick up?"

"I dunno. I just swipe things. I don't read 'em."

"Nobody move," said a new voice. "Hands up."

The trio turned to face a tall black man. His bulk filled the hall doorway. He wore the uniform of the TecLab security force.

And he had a pistol pointed at them.

Chapter 17: Midnight Confessions

Noelle's arms shot straight up in surrender. Destiny turned to face the man and raised her hands shoulder high. The kid bolted for the open window. The security guard fired; the blast echoed around the room. The bullet nicked the burglar in a shoulder, but he kept going. He dove through the open window, leaving droplets of blood behind, and hot footed down the ladder.

"Just a flesh wound," Destiny observed. "He'll get away."

The man glanced at the closed safe. "But he didn't get what he come after." He moved toward the women, with the gun leveled at them. "And neither will you."

"Don't shoot us, please, Tony," Noelle begged. The man glared at her. She squinted and lowered her arms slightly. "You're not Tony."

"Shut up!" he yelled.

Destiny looked at Noelle, puzzled. The actress explained. "Dad told me there's only one black man on the company security team and that's Tony. I've met Tony, and you're not him."

"Good work spotting an imposter, Tabby Gray," said Destiny. "Who are you, mister?"

"You." He pointed the gun at Destiny. "Open the safe."

She turned coy to stall for time. "For real? I don't know the combination, bro."

"Then you better figure it out, girl, before I shoot off your pretty little face."

Destiny tiled her head. "Now you wouldn't want to do that, would you? I mean, we could work together to get what we both want." She took a hard look at the man. "Say, I know your voice. You're the guy we saw talking to Old Scratch on the park bench couple of days ago."

He lowered the gun just a bit. "How do you know about that?"

Destiny gave a girlish giggle. "There's a lot you don't know about me, bro."

As they were talking, Noelle glanced around for a means of escape. She spotted the desk lamp the kid had turned on. The fake guard had his attention focused on Destiny, giving Noelle a chance to slowly scoot closer to the desk. She stretched out a foot while keeping her arms up. She hooked the toe of her shoe around the cord and yanked. The lamp crashed onto the floor. The light bulb broke with a loud pop, and the broken glass scattered everywhere. The man was distracted long enough for Destiny to leap and plant both palms on his chest. She pushed him to the ground. He landed on his back with a thud. She kicked the gun from his hand and then straddled him, grabbing his wrists and pressing them to the floor.

"All right, who are you?" she demanded.

From the hallway came the sound of the elevator gears grinding and a "ding" as the cab reached the floor.

"The real security guards!" Destiny shouted. "Tabby Gray! Out the window!"

She didn't need to tell her partner twice. Noelle darted to the window, and stumbled none too gracefully through the opening. Destiny punched the guy in the face to stop him from following them. She grabbed the burglar's backpack and followed Noelle. Fortunately, the kid had been in such a rush that he'd left the rope in place—or it would have been a long jump down four stories.

Noelle scrambled down the ladder. The thin cords swayed, and she felt none too secure. She took one quick glance down, which made her dizzy. She stopped.

Density's foot landed on Noelle's head. "Get a move on it!"

Noelle took a deep breath and continued her descent, hurrying to keep ahead of Destiny. The women reached the ground just as a clanging alarm bell deafened them—the real guards had found the imposter. The spies crouched low and ducked behind a bush just as guards ran from the building. The women circled around the facility, using the trees as cover. Clouds covered the moon, providing shadows for the women to hide in.

They reached the area where they had hidden the jetpacks. This time Noelle put on her own jetpack. The guards approached; one of them ordered the spies to stop. The women fired up their respective jetpacks and flew into the sky. The guards fired. The bullets missed the women's feet as they soared. The spies were over the wall in a flash. They jumped into the SIAMESE car and sped away. At a safe distance, Destiny pulled over so the women could remove the uncomfortable jetpacks and dump them in the back seat. Then they continue on their way.

"I hope Dad doesn't find out I was here tonight," Noelle said.

"The guards couldn't see our faces in the dark," said Destiny. "And the faker isn't about to rat on us. He'd never admit that a couple of chicks outsmarted him. The guards wouldn't believe him anyway. The ladder isn't ours, so they can't ID us with that."

"Where to now? Find the kid who broke in?"

Destiny shook her head. "He won't lead us to Old Scratch. He's on the lam in the other direction. Old

Scratch isn't nice to the people who fail him. Besides, the twerp's small potatoes. We want the cash crop."

"So, he was telling the truth about being a burglar?"

"Right on, sister."

Destiny parked at Noelle's house. She said they needed to talk before she turned in her report to Hanover. Inside the secure and warm cottage, Noelle offered Destiny something to drink.

"I don't suppose you have any scotch or gin?" Destiny asked.

"Sorry, no. I don't keep booze."

"I was afraid of that."

"How about some hot cocoa? I could use something to warm me up."

"Suit yourself."

Destiny sank onto the living room sofa while Noelle lit a burner on the kitchenette's gas range. She filled a pan with milk, sugar, powered cocoa and vanilla, and stirred while it heated. She poured the steaming cocoa into two ceramic mugs and dropped a handful of marshmallows into both cups. She gave one mug to Destiny and set the other on a table coaster before she went to the bedroom to change clothes. She soon returned, dressed in a blue Indiana State University sweatshirt and sweatpants.

Ceebee was curled on Destiny's lap. Noelle smiled and nodded at the cat. "I'm being snubbed in my own house." She sat down in the easy chair and took a sip of her cocoa. "Why did we run if we had Old Scratch cornered?"

"Because we didn't. Old Scratch would have just shot us or forced us to open the safe without any dumb chitchat. By the way, nice footwork with the lamp."

"Thanks. I remember what you said the last time about making a distraction when someone has the drop on us."

"You learn quick. Remember on our last mission when I said we had a wild card? We got both the Ruskies and another player after the same thing. Only the wild card is an amateur, and amateurs are dangerous, because you don't know what they're going to do. A real spy, I know what they're thinking."

"What do we do now? The plan failed."

"Not really. We know your cousin's broadcast worked. And we still got an ace we can play. Old Scratch thinks the blueprints are real. He doesn't know that we don't have them. We can pretend that we got the goods and sell them on the open market."

"Sounds good, except for one thing. We don't have Old Scratch's phone number to call and tell him we got the plans that don't exist."

"Good point," said Destiny.

"I could ask Mamie to do another fake broadcast for us."

"You can't use the same ruse twice." She picked up the backpack. "Let's see if the kid left us a clue."

Destiny pushed aside the piles of magazines and mail atop the coffee table and dumped out the contents of the burglar's backpack. Inside the kit they found safecracking tools, a map of the plant's fourth floor and a flashlight as well as one unexpected item: one of the brochures the SPARK devotees handed out at their rallies.

Destiny picked up the pamphlet, and the women locked eyes.

"Looks like it's time for the Wise One to tell us what he knows." The veteran spy tossed the pamphlet on the table and picked up the receiver of the Princess telephone. "Is your phone secure?"

Noelle nodded. Destiny dialed the SIAMESE number and was soon talking to Hanover. Noelle leaned over in an effort to overhear the conversation.

At one point Destiny covered the mouthpiece with her hand. "Hanover wants to know if you can do a Russian accent."

Noelle's brow wrinkled in confusion. "Why? Does he want me to defect?"

Chapter 18: I'm A Believer

Noelle's usual Sunday morning habit included church and Sunday School at Old Beth church, but this morning her plans changed. Before Destiny had left the house, she'd outlined Hanover's plan for trapping Old Scratch. Noelle had some dirty work to do before the SPARK rally that afternoon in Yuletide's Poinsettia Park, including a visit to the True Believers' worship service to look for redheads and find out what the congregation knew about Blossom's death.

Over a breakfast of bacon, eggs and a brown sugar cinnamon Pop-Tart, she prayed aloud. "God, I'm sorry for missing church, but I hope you understand. I have to save the country and catch a murderer. And I'll be in church next Sunday, promise." She turned on the radio and listened to one of the morning gospel services as she ate. Not the same as being in her own church, but it'd do.

After feeding Ceebee and letting him outside to play, she dug out her language tapes. In college she had worked with the acting teacher to develop accents for the stage. At long last she had the opportunity to put her studies to work—for real. How well she could pull this off would not result in a rave from a critic, but life or death for many people. She found the Russian language cassette, which she popped into her portable tape player. Seated at the kitchenette table, Noelle spoke along with the tape to work up a realistic Russian accent. With the limited rehearsal time, she wouldn't fool a native Russian, but she could get by in a pinch.

When she finished with the language work, Noelle put on a plaid shirt, blue jeans, loafers and a sweater. She drove to the alley behind the town's liquor store for a necessary task that she loathed to do. The people she needed to see would be hanging out there. She parked behind the store so no one driving down the street would see her car. She found her target: a gang of greasy-haired guys was shooting craps against the back wall of the liquor store. The only reason they were outside the building instead of inside was that the store was closed Sundays. Their motorcycles were lined up along the other side of the alley. The guys, all dressed in leather jackets, white T-shirts, jeans and cowboy boots, were smoking. As she walked up, they stopped their dice game. Noelle coughed and waved aside the cigarette smoke.

"Well, lookie who's here!" Vince was the leader of the town's bad boys, a bunch of adult ne're-do-wells who scrapped by on odd jobs. They had no purpose in life other than to drink, shoot pool, cause trouble and look at girlie magazines. Vince's dark hair was loaded with Brylcream in an attempt to mimic Elvis' pompadour.

"If it ain't Goody Two-Shoes McNabb come to visit us this fine Sunday morning. Hey, how come you're not church?"

"Why aren't you? A good dose of religion would clean you up," she retorted.

Vince glanced at the guys and they all chuckled. "Did you come here to evangelize and get us saved?"

"You could use a good talking to, but that'll have to wait. I need a favor from you guys."

The men glanced at each other and laughed suggestively.

"Not *that* kind of favor," she said. "Now, listen." Noelle briefly explained the plan, ending with, "All I want is a diversion. Don't break anything or hurt anyone. If you tear up the property or run over someone, you won't get paid."

"Paid, huh?" said Vince. "How much."

"Twenty dollars apiece, in cash." Too much money for these bums, but SIAMESE was footing the bill.

The men whistled in appreciation. "Where's the dough?" Vince asked.

"You get half now, and half when the job's finished. The deal depends on you keeping your traps shut. I was never here this morning, and you never talked to me."

"Sounds copasetic. What's behind this scheme, anyway? Why do you want us to do this?"

"Never mind. I'm not paying you to think. If I were, it'd only cost me a nickel."

Noelle and Vince shook hands on the deal. She handed him a plain white envelope filled with cash. She hurried to her car and sped away. Every time she spoke with the slimy Vince, she felt like she needed to shower afterwards, which she did once she got home. Noelle changed into a nice Sunday morning dress—something knee length, not her usual miniskirt—pantyhose and heels for her next assignment.

But before putting on her gloves and hat, Noelle decided she needed a disguise. Yuletide was a small town, and she didn't want word to get out that she was chummy around with the True Believers crowd. She still had her makeup case from her college plays. Seated at the dressing table in the bedroom, Noelle switched on the lighted mirror. She slapped on some light foundation, pink lipstick and pale blue eye shadow with a touch of eye liner, not as heavy as how she usually wore. Noelle pulled on a shorthaired wig with traces of gray that made her look older. She slipped on a pair of tortoise-rim, cat's-eye spectacles with clear glass lenses that she had used in a production of *Our Town*. She'd stay at the back of the sanctuary and hope that nobody would notice her.

The True Believers Congregation didn't own a huge, ornate building like Old Beth. Rather, the sect met in a tiny, plain white building, a former pizza parlor that had gone out of business. Noelle parked her car a few blocks away from the church, on a residential street in case anyone recognized her Bug. The white building resembled the other stores along the street save for a small wooden sign nailed beside the front door that listed the group's name and the Sunday service time. Noelle climbed the short flight of steps that led to the front door. Once inside, she glanced around to get her bearings.

A white-haired man in dark suit and tie seemed to appear out of nowhere and, before she could object, he firmly shook her hand. "Welcome! So glad to have you with us!"

Noelle forced a smile. She hadn't counted on anyone talking to her. She'd hoped to slip in unnoticed. But in such a small gathering, a stranger stood out like a dandelion in new mowed grass.

"What's your name?" he asked.

"Suzie. Suzie Smith." She struggled to free her hand from the enveloping grip.

"That's great! Your first time here?"

"Uh, yes."

"How did you hear about us?"

Her mind was so jumbled she blurted, "The newspaper." Blast! How stupid! Now the cult would keep on running their dreadful advertisements.

"May I take your coat?" The man grabbed the shoulders of her garment.

Noelle pulled the front of her coat tight. "Ah, no thanks. I'll keep it on. I'm a bit chilly." Actually, she was warm in the overheated building, but she wanted to keep her things close at hand in case she needed to make a quick getaway.

"You live around here?"

"No, I'm visiting from out of town." Just in case he tried to look her up in the local phone book. But Noelle worried that she was getting good at lying. She was never this way before her involvement with SIAMESE. "Where's the ladies room?" Noelle didn't have to go, but she wanted an excuse to flee from the pest.

"Downstairs in the basement. But let me show you to your seat first. We'll be starting soon."

The man grabbed her arm and pulled her into the adjacent room that she assumed was the sanctuary. But instead of wood pews, thick carpeting and stained-glass windows, the room contained metal folding chairs, a tile floor and windows covered with frayed curtains. The room couldn't hold more than a hundred people, and only a fourth of the seats were filled. The air reeked of a stinky room freshener meant to cover odors. The usher marched her down the center aisle so everyone could see her. He directed her to the front row.

"Oh, excuse me," Noelle said. "I'd rather sit in the back." The man eyed her. "I'm far sighted. I see better at a distance."

Noelle slipped her arm from the usher's grip, hurried to the back row and plopped herself in an aisle seat so nobody could block her in. Besides staying hidden in the back row, Noelle could scan the audience for red heads. She spotted one family—a man, woman and three squirmy kids—all with dark red hair. Perhaps Clement was wrong about a red-headed man renting the boat. Some hair colors look different in the sunlight. But even if Clement was right, what could she do? Noelle couldn't walk up to the family and ask if they had recently taken a girl's life.

The front of the room had a carpeted platform with a podium in the middle, a spinet piano to one side and a projection screen on the other side. The wall behind the platform had a door to one side and a large hanging banner that read, "Right Belief Is Right Living." The door opened, and a two people walked out onto the stage. An elderly woman took her place at the piano and shuffled some battered hymnals that were perched on the music holder. A huge man followed her. The man's bulk was muscle, not fat. He could have easily taken down Quarterback Whitlock in his prime. The buttons on his white shirt, stretched across his chest, threatened to pop off. His shoulders, broad enough to carry a yoke, were held high and back. His spine was straight as an arrow. From the top of his bald head to his shiny, black leather shoes, the man moved like a god used to crowds parting before him.

The bald head—of course! Maybe the killer wore a toupee to hide his identity. But wouldn't a hat be a better disguise? After all, red hair was so rare that people were bound to remember it. But maybe the murderer wanted to throw people off his track with a distinct look.

"Good morning, all. For any newcomers, I'm Brother Gideon." With his strong voice, the pastor didn't need a microphone. He rambled on about the beautiful weather and the joy of coming together on the Lord's day. The seated members gazed at the speaker with rapt attention, save for a couple of parents trying to quiet their kids.

"Do we have any visitors with us today?" he asked.

Noelle slid down in her chair to hide behind the person sitting in front of her, but to no avail. The usher stood behind her and clapped his boney fingers on her shoulders.

"We have Suzie Smith with us today," he announced.

Brother Gideon grinned. "Let's give Miss Smith a warm True Believers welcome!"

The congregation turned to gawk at her and clap. Normally Noelle relished the sound of audience applause, but today she wanted to disappear. She offered back a wan smile.

Brother Gideon beamed at her. "I'm looking forward to getting to know Miss Smith better after the service."

Noelle wasn't sure what he meant by that. Was he expecting some hanky panky in the parsonage? Shame on her for even thinking such thoughts. None too soon, the usher released his grip on her and moved away. Brother Gideon sat in one of the chairs in the front row. Another man took his place at the podium and announced it was time for worship. Someone in the back of the room turned on an overhead projector. On the screen flashed the words of the first hymn. The pianist pounded the tinny instrument with all her might as the congregation joined the music leader in singing "A Mighty Fortress is Our God." The group continued with a few more hymns as someone changed the plastic word sheets on the projector. Noelle loved singing at her church, but the large choir and talented organist at Old Beth had spoiled her. Here, she had the urge to stick her fingers in her ears. At one point a crying child thankfully drowned out the racket. Finally, the music stopped.

Brother Gideon rose to preach. He didn't stand behind the podium but paced the front of the room, speaking without notes. His voice rose in a stream of judgment against SPARK, how they were following Satan and destroying the nation by brainwashing the young.

Brother Gideon shook his fist as he roared. "God's holy word will not be mocked! He will destroy all infidels by his mighty hand! We are God's hands, and it's our calling to remove this plague from the face of the earth until all believe the true word of God!"

He announced that the church was planning a counter-rally at the SPARK event that afternoon in the park. Noelle perked up.

"We must rid our town of this heresy," he said. "We invite all of you to join us. There's strength in numbers. We must warn our community. We'll use the sword of God to strike down the infidels and drive them out of town!"

Did Brother Gideon mean what he said? Did he intend to remove the devotees by killing them? With his intensity he could easily rile up his followers into a mob—one that could wreck havoc at the afternoon rally. After ten more minutes, Noelle could no longer stand the tirade. Brother Gideon's voice, amplified by the bare walls, grated on her ears. Noelle waited until the usher was tending to a child on the opposite side of the room, and then she bolted through the door at the back of the room. She raced out the front door and down the steps, not stopping until she reached her car. Whew! No pedestrians on the street, so nobody knew about her brief visit with the True Believers. Noelle zipped home so she could change clothes and meet up with Destiny. She had to warn her partner that they might need to deal with Brother Gideon at the rally.

Chapter 19: The Happening

Destiny and Noelle, disguised again in their hippie personas, showed up for the rally around noon at Poinsettia Park. The wig made Noelle's scalp itch, and she still had difficulty seeing through the tinted glasses. She was afraid that someone from the Riverbend rally might recognize them, but Destiny assured her that they would keep out of sight of the crowd and then split once the mission was accomplished. The weather was cooperating for the event: slightly cloudy but no rain, and warmer temperatures that didn't require coats.

The normally quiet park, wooded with mature oak and elm trees, was bustling with activity. Multiple chartered buses lined the streets, dropping off devotees from out of town. Curious residents from nearby towns arrived, eager to take part in any unusual activity that might add some sparkle to their routine rural lives. Even the tourists bypassed the theme park to take in the spectacle. Yuletide residents stood along the edges of the park, eyeing the crowd with concern. A few kids romped on the playground equipment, oblivious to the adult activity around them. The devotees filled the park—dancing, singing and banging on tambourines. Wise One's throne had been set up inside the gazebo, along with smaller chairs for First Sage and the town mayor, who was participating reluctantly in the event at SPARK's invitation. First Sage felt the mayor's presence would add validity to the event. Chris Kloss thought his attendance might ease the tensions between the townsfolk and the intruders. However, Kloss made sure he showed up in a suit and tie, not his Santa suit.

Destiny and Noelle stood in a clump of trees where they could watch but not be seen. Destiny leaned over and spoke softly to Noelle. "We're in trouble."

"What's wrong?"

"The fuzz is here."

Some Yuletide police offices were stationed throughout the park.

"We'll be okay," said Noelle. "They're more amused than alert. They think this'll be a walk in the park for some easy overtime."

"Won't they be surprised. We'll have to move fast before they have time to react. Brother Gideon and his gang, where are they?"

"I'll have a look around."

Destiny handed her the comb radio. "When you find them, call me. Don't try to take down any crazies on your own."

Noelle made her way along the fringes of the crowd and turned her head away whenever she recognized someone. She didn't need her cover blown. Noelle reached the main park entrance and found the feared mob of True Believers—or rather, a handful of people standing around a card table. A poster set up on the table read "Let US Show You the True Way to Salvation" with "US" in red to stand among the black letters. On the table stood stacks of pamphlets with such titles as "Only One Way into Heaven," "The Truth about SPARK" and "Busting Myths about The Bible." The church members handed out the brochures to everyone entering the park. Some people took the papers and stuffed them into a jacket pocket to read later; others dropped the leaflets into the nearby trashcan. The evangelizers were persistent, but quiet and non-aggressive.

Brother Gideon had changed from his bluster of the morning. He smiled, shook hands, patted children on the head, and was civil to the guests. What had happened to the fire and brimstone of the sermon? Or was that just an act to get his small flock motivated?

The preacher shoved a pamphlet into the hand of a guest. "Here, take the sword of God and read it. The words will cut through the fakery you'll be hearing here."

Noelle slapped her forehead. Of course! The sword of God! The pastor's sermon did not refer to a literal weapon, but to the scriptures. How could she be so dense, fretting over nothing. Perhaps the True Believers were just as harmless as SPARK seemed to be.

Just a few yards away, the SPARK devotees were handing out *their* pamphlets to the same folk who had picked up literature from the True Believers table. A battle of beliefs. Noelle smiled—until she saw Brother Gideon approaching Chakra.

"Young man! Young man!" the clergyman called.

What did he have in mind? Noelle inched closer so she could hear. She hid behind the World Wars monument and pressed a button on her comb radio. "Black Manx, we might have a situation here at the front gate."

"Hang tight," Destiny replied. "On my way."

Brother Gideon reached his target as Noelle watched. "Young man, I need to speak with you."

Chakra ran his eyes over the preacher. He didn't look happy to see him. "Yeah, man, get with the words. What's your beef?"

"Young man, I'm terribly worried about your soul."

Chakra glanced at the other devotees gathered around him and laughed. "Hey, dude, nothing' wrong with my soul! I'm free as a bird and feelin' groovy."

"If you were to die right now, would you end up in hell or in heaven?"

"If I bunk much longer in Yuletide, that sure won't be heaven!"

"I am quite serious." Indeed, Brother Gideon sounded concerned, more like a friend than an accuser. "I had a son. Apple of my eye. I taught him the right way, raised him properly, but he rebelled and sinned. He left his home and the church. One day he died in a terrible automobile accident. He was about your age when he passed." The preacher's voice softened. "You see, young man, I would hate for you to lose out on eternity if you were to suffer a similar fate."

Chakra said to Brother Gideon. "Yo, man, I can dig where you're coming from." He reached out and took the preacher's hand in his. "That stinks when the good die young. I bet your kid was a great guy."

Tears welled in Brother Gideon's eyes. "He was."

Destiny slipped up beside Noelle. "What's happening?"

"Apparently nothing."

The loudspeakers set up around the park crackled as they warmed up. Over the speakers came the thump of someone's finger tapping a microphone to see if it was turned on. Brother Gideon and Chakra broke their grip and moved in separate directions, once more passing out their respective fliers to the passers-by.

Kloss' voice rang out across the area. "Ladies and gentlemen . . . " He paused as feedback whined through the amps. "Ladies and gentlemen and guests to our fair city, welcome. If you would please gather in front of the gazebo, the rally will be starting soon. Oh, and the organizers of the event have asked that there be no smoking on the grounds during their presentation. Thank you."

Destiny and Noelle hurried to a wooded area behind the gazebo, where the camper from the Riverbend rally was parked. The psychedelic

SIAMESE van was close by but hidden behind the building that contained the public restrooms. Two agents alit from the SIAMESE vehicle. The burly middle-age men looked ludicrous in their hippie garb— ripped blue jeans, tight-fitting tie-dye shirts and ill-fitting wigs of long black hair that they kept pushing out of their faces.

"Dash should have sent over some younger guys," Noelle observed.

"It's a delicate operation with split-second timing," said Density. "Hanover wanted veterans working the mission. Are you sure your guys will show up?"

"I paid Vince the bribe money you gave me. He's greedy enough to do it."

First Sage stepped up to a podium that had been placed in the gazebo. He grasped the edges of the podium and leaned into the microphone.

"Gather round, children. The Wise One has deemed us worthy to bless us with his presence and his wisdom."

The devotees cheered and clustered tightly in front of the gazebo. The out-of-town visitors set up folding chairs farther back and settled in to watch. Noelle didn't see Blossom's former boyfriend or Marlo from the bowling alley. She hoped their absence was by choice and not because someone from SPARK had detained them. The Yuletide residents stayed as far from the devotees as they could, but they still seemed attentive. The True Believers packed up their handouts, folded up their table, and left. They didn't want to hear the Wise One, but at least they had the courtesy not to remain and interrupt his talk. The police counted the minutes until they could go to their homes and maybe catch the final quarter of a ball game on TV.

The mayor took a seat on the platform as First Sage launched into an overblown speech, quoting passages from SPARK writings to hype the devotees for the Wise One's appearance, and bore everyone else to death. The SIAMESE agents waited unseen behind the bandstand.

First Sage reached a high peak of excitement. "And now, for all the faithful who seek meaning and purpose from life, for all whose hearts burn with the fire of love and peace, please give a rousing welcome to our guide and counselor, our learned leader, the Wise One!"

First Sage sat in the stage right chair. The devotees erupted into a fever pitch of screams and cheers, applauding and madly whacking their tambourines. Noelle had never heard such ecstasy, outside of a rock concert or the night the Yuletide High School Elves basketball team won the sectional championship. Wise One left the camper, assisted by a male devotee. The escort held Wise One's arms and helped him up the gazebo stairs, one step at a time. Wise One shuffled to the podium. The escort adjusted the microphone for the right height. The followers' frenzy increased at the sight of their loved one. Wise One stood at the front of the platform, waved his hands in blessing over the crowd, and nodded at the devotees. The escort left the stage. Wise One motioned for the crowd to quiet down. An eerie hush fell over the spectators. Noelle caught her breath, anxious to hear.

Then Wise One spoke, and Noelle understood his power. His voice was soft, yet his words were clearly articulated. A slight East Indian accent added charm to his speech. He spoke with gentleness and authority. Love and acceptance seemed to ooze out of him. Noelle found herself caught up in his words, so much so that she wanted to call off the mission and stay behind to listen. No wonder the devotees loved him.

Destiny checked her wristwatch and gave Noelle a glance: *Where are they?* Noelle shrugged. If the bad boys didn't arrive soon, the mission was off.

Just as the Wise One said, "Shall we pray," came a distant roar of motorcycles.

The townsfolk were used to the bad boys cruising Kringle Avenue; at first, they paid no mind. The sound grew louder. Those standing on the farthest edges of park perked up at the sound. Vince and his pals tore into the park astride their high-handlebar choppers. The bad boys left the service road that led to the parking lot, veering onto the grassy area and heading straight for the crowd. The bystanders screamed and jumped out of the way. The bikers split into different directions, coming close enough to scare but not to strike anyone. The lethargic cops, lured to complacency by the soothing talk, woke up and chased the bikers, yelling at them to stop. But the overweight men on foot were no match for the motorcycles. The bikers whooped it up as they circled the lawn.

The interruption alarmed Wise One, who waved his arms. "Oh, please, please, let us have peace!"

Mayor Kloss jumped to his feet and pushed Wise One aside so he could use the microphone. "Attention! Will the men on the motorbikes please leave the park immediately!" But nobody heard him over the whine of the hogs.

With all eyes on the bikers, the agents launched their scheme. Destiny handed an air filter to Noelle to put on as she slipped one over her own nose and mouth. Noelle found the device bulky and uncomfortable, but necessary. The two male agents, who also wore face filters, slipped up behind the gazebo and threw gas pellets onto the floor of the bandstand. A thick, black smoke from the pellets enveloped the space. Due to the knockout gas, Wise One and Chris collapsed to the floor. First Sage slumped, unconscious, in his chair. The smoke hid the male agents as they ran up the steps. One agent picked up Wise One and threw him over one shoulder; the second man did the same with First Sage. They rushed down the steps and to the van. Destiny yanked open the back door of the van, and the men deposited their cargo into the back of the vehicle. The agents got into the cab. Destiny and Noelle piled into the back of the vehicle and locked the door behind them. The van pulled away and hit Kringle Avenue as the smoke on the bandstand began to clear.

Someone in the park spotted the empty chairs and screamed. The police ran to the gazebo and attempted to wake up the mayor, who remained in a deep slumber. The bikers roared out of the park, their job finished, and headed out of town to a deserted barn for an afternoon of drinking and hiding from the cops. But for now, those present were more concerned about the missing persons than the rowdy hotheads.

Inside the van, Destiny pulled off her air filter and Noelle did the same. Noelle took a breath of fresh air and nodded at the men, who were sound asleep on the floor. "Can they hear us?"

"No, they'll be out until we give them the wake-up drug." Destiny began to remove her disguise.

"What about the mayor? Will he be all right?"

"My guess is he usually takes a siesta on Sunday afternoons. He should be awake in time for his supper." Destiny slid open a narrow panel in the back door and peered out. "Nobody's following us. So far, so good."

"I told you Vince and his gang would come through."

"Lucky for you, they did. Otherwise, Hanover would have your hide for a rug on his office floor."

The van arrived at SIAMESE headquarters; Noelle could tell because of the sudden dip as the vehicle headed down the underground entry ramp. Inside the underground parking lot, Destiny and Noelle jumped out of the vehicle. Other agents brought in stretchers to carry away the unconscious prisoners. After Destiny and Noelle entered the facility and put on their ID badges, the spy escorted the actress two levels down to the wardrobe department. Other women agents dressed the actress in a brown, long-sleeved jacket with a high collar along with a below-the-knee shirt. The black pencil skirt only allowed Noelle to take small steps; at least the flat shoes were easy to walk in. The makeup experts fitted her with a black wig with a tight bun. The agents washed the temporary tattoo off Noelle's check and applied foundation to make her face paler, lipstick to darken her lips and black eyeliner to make her eyes look more severe. A pair of glasses with clear glass lenses and thick black plastic frames completed the ensemble. This must be what happens at a movie studio, when people dress and fuss over a star. But this was no play-acting for film—lives were at stake in this drama.

Destiny took Noelle to the "stage" where she would act out the scene. A room in SIAMESE headquarters had been transformed into a replica of a Russian KGB office, with a Soviet Union flag in one corner, a portrait of Lenin on one wall and a large map of the United States with colored pins set in strategic cities on another wall.

Noelle spun around to take in the enclosed set. "This is incredible! SIAMESE built this overnight?"

"We got specs on file of just about every kind of government installation in Europe and Asia," said Destiny.

"I feel lost without you. I wish you were doing this too."

"You'll be a hit. Dash should be here any minute." Destiny tucked Noelle's security badge inside her blouse. "Keep that thing hidden. It's a dead giveaway. Good luck."

Destiny left just as Hanover entered the door. Noelle gasped. He looked every inch a Russian officer, from his highly polished black shoes, black suit and tie, to his dyed blond hair. An insignia with the hammer-and-sickle was pinned to his lapel. A slight bulge beneath his jacket betrayed a shoulder holster. Was he planning to use his gun? He stopped in front of Noelle and looked her over with a critical eye. She swallowed.

"Good, good," he said. "Let me hear your accent."

Noelle thought back to her Russian language tapes. "Welcome, comrade. We are happy that you could join us for the investigation."

"That's fine. You sit here." He indicated a chair behind a small table that held a large reel-to-reel tape recorder. Beside the chair and table stood an imposing oak desk for Hanover's role. Noelle took a seat at the table.

"Your role is to turn on the tape recorder. You will also fetch coffee if I request it."

"What do I say?"

"Very little. Russian women are generally seen and not heard. But I wanted you to brush up on the accent just in case. A glitch can occur in even the best-planned schemes."

"Won't First Sage recognize me?"

"Not if you play your part well. People see what they expect to see. Besides, the targets will be groggy and disoriented from the drug. We can use that to our advantage."

The desk phone rang; Hanover picked it up. "Yes?" He listened and then hung up. "There's a slight delay. The targets will arrive shortly. We can relax until then. Coffee?"

"No, thank you." Noelle was so nervous that anything she drank would send her running for a bathroom.

Hanover opened the desk drawer, removed a cardboard packet of Belomorkanal cigarettes, and picked up a metal lighter from the desktop. He tapped the open packet against his hand, removed one of the Russian cigarettes, and lit it.

Noelle watched, amazed at learning something new about the mystery man. "I didn't know you smoked."

He exhaled a long stream of smoke and eyed her. "I've smoked for fifteen years, and enjoyed every puff."

She tried not to cough from the smell of the strong tobacco. "Do you get nervous on these missions when you don't know what the targets will do or say?"

"I suppose no more than you do waiting in the wings before going on stage for a play."

Hanover took another puff. He looked so calm, so collected. Didn't anything faze this guy? He seemed preoccupied, perhaps turning over the mission plan in his mind, but Noelle wanted to talk. A certain matter had been bubbling up inside her for some time.

"Mr. Hanover, may I ask you a personal question?"

He studied a stack of papers on the desktop instead of looking at her. "Why?"

"Why hasn't your mother gotten in touch with my mother?"

Hanover froze and looked at her. She braced herself for an explosion. Noelle tried to read his face, but Dash was an expert in masking his feelings.

"Why would she want to do that?" he said.

"Because they're sisters."

Hanover's eyes blazed. He ground the end of the cigarette into the ashtray on the desk. "My family is of no concern to you."

"It's my family too. I want to meet my aunt."

"Impossible." He stepped over to the wall and stared at the map, hands behind his back.

"Mr. Hanover, I don't know what you're trying to hide, but my mom very much wants to see her sister again. Even if my aunt did something monstrous in the past, mom's ready to forgive her and—"

He turned. "You were not to know about our relationship."

"Well, I do. I don't know why you're ashamed of it."

He stormed to where Noelle sat, placed his palms flat on the tabletop, and leaned over the table to speak to her. "I am concerned for my safety and yours. If our enemies found out about our connection, your family would be a target. Our foes would try to get to me through them and destroy all of us, along with the entire apparatus. SIAMESE is unauthorized and clandestine. The CIA, the Russians and terrorist syndicates want to shut us down. The work we do is too important to jeopardize over sentimentality."

"You're good at keeping secrets. Why can't you arrange a meeting, just one time, here in headquarters between mom and Aunt Grizelda and me? Nobody else would know."

Hanover straightened up. His voice was low and menacing. "Have you considered that your aunt might not want to see you?"

The question kicked Noelle in the gut. Her eyes watered. She removed the glasses and wiped her eyes with the back of her hand. The thought of another family member shunning her was too hard to take.

Hanover crossed the room and, with his back to Noelle, covered his face with his hands and took a deep breath. Then he stood by the desk and lit another cigarette, his hands shaking. He had no choice but to lie to Noelle. She must not know the ugly secrets about his mother. Protecting their families was paramount—even if Noelle despised him for doing so.

Chapter 20: Back in the USSR

The sharp ring of the desk phone shattered the silence.

Hanover picked up the phone, his voice as calm as ever. "Yes? Good. We're ready." He hung up and went to Noelle. He pulled out a handkerchief from his pocket and fixed the tear-smeared makeup on her face. "All right now. Focus on the mission. It's show time." Hanover put back the hanky, sat behind the desk, and glanced at Noelle. "Are you set?"

She pushed the glasses back on her nose and prayed that the tobacco smoke drifting her way didn't choke her. "Yes. I'm ready."

A knock came from the outer door. Hanover's eyes turned a cold, steely gray. He sat ramrod straight in the chair and disappeared into his character. "Come."

The door opened. Two SIAMESE agents, dressed as Russian soldiers and holding rifles, marched in, with Wise One and First Sage between them. Hanover nodded at the two straight-backed chairs facing the desk.

"Sit." His Russian accent was impeccable.

The soldiers guided the prisoners into the armless chairs. Wise One and First Sage gazed around, mouths ajar. First Sage fingered a rope of wooden prayer beads.

Wise One clasped his hands tightly, fingers interlocked. "Oh, dear. Oh, dear. Oh, dear," he muttered.

Hanover rolled his padded office chair close to the desk and rested his elbows on the desktop blotter. He held the cigarette lightly between his raised fingers, and the smoke drifted upward.

"Greetings, comrades. I am Major Boris Krovopuskov of the KGB. This is," he nodded at Noelle, "Lieutenant Natasha Bogomolov, my assistant."

First Sage licked his lips. "I—I am—"

"Yes, we know who you are. We will now begin." He pointed at Noelle. She switched on the tape recorder. "Your regular handler has turned both of you over to me. He said you were being, shall we say, uncooperative."

"We don't understand," said First Sage. "What do you want of us? Where are we?"

"You are in the central Midwest American command post of the Soviet secret intelligence. We brought you here because we're unhappy at how you mishandled your last assignment."

"What are you talking about? We know nothing about the Russians. We are simple sojourners seeking the path to eternal joy."

"Please, you can drop your pious act with me. We have no time for that."

"I am who I am and nobody more. Why are we here? We've done nothing wrong."

"That depends." Hanover took a long draw on the cigarette and blew the smoke toward the targets. "Would you prefer that I call you by your code name? Old Scratch?"

"That is not my name," said First Sage.

Hanover's lips tightened. He tapped the end of his cigarette on the ashtray. Noelle could sense his frustration. The interrogation was not going the way Dash had planned.

"Coffee?" Hanover asked.

"We do not drink stimulants of any kind," said First Sage.

"That is strange. The last time you met with your handler, you drank coffee."

"Who is this handler you keep talking about?"

Hanover looked at Noelle. "One coffee."

"Yes, major." She marched to the carafe and soon had a cup of lukewarm coffee on Hanover's desk before returning to her seat.

"We will try this again," said Dash. He placed the cigarette in the ashtray and rested his forearms on the desk. He wrapped his hands around the coffee cup, but didn't drink. "What is your name?"

First Sage twisted the beads around his hand. "Do you mean before I joined SPARK? I was Joss Benningham. I studied philosophy in college. I wrote my thesis on world religions. After college I sold shoes while I investigated metaphysical and Eastern thought. After my college studies, I knew many things except the path to serenity. I found that when I met the Wise One. I believe in his mystical vision. I came to him as a humble devotee and, despite my unworthiness, Wise One elevated me to my current duties."

Hanover said, "The plans to the new American defense missile. Where are they? You were instructed to turn the plans over to us. Are you planning to sell them to another country?"

First Sage shrugged. His voice rose in pitch and shook. "We know nothing about missiles. We are peace loving. We abhor violence of all kinds."

Hanover took a pencil from the pencil holder, leaned back in his chair, and tapped the pencil on the desk blotter for a few moments. Tap . . . tap . . . tap. . . . The room was silent save for the steady rap of the pencil and the whirl of the tape machine.

"I am a busy man. I have no patience with stubborn agents." First Sage only stared at Hanover. Dash pointed the pencil at Wise One. "That one, does he talk?"

First Sage replied. "His voice is a sacred instrument. The Wise One only speaks when it is necessary to impart spiritual guidance."

Hanover rose and sat on the front of his desk. "Old Scratch, you hired a young cat burglar to break into the Werner TecLab in Yuletide and steal the plans for the new missile."

"No, no, never," said First Sage. "You have us confused with someone else. We're innocent."

"Is that so?" Hanover opened a manila file on the desktop, removed the SPARK brochure that had been in the crook's bag, and handled the leaflet to First Sage. "Your thief had this on him during the burglary. How did it get there unless you gave it to him?"

First Sage browsed the brochure and looked pleadingly at Hanover. "We give out thousands of these pamphlets. This young man could have picked it up from anywhere."

"How much did you pay this man to steal for you?"

"Nothing, nothing. Thievery is wrong. That builds up bad karma. Oh, please, let us go. We cannot tell you whatever it is that you wish to hear."

"Tell me about your other plans. The other secrets you have stolen from your country."

First Sage did not reply. He folded his hands, closed his eyes, and touched his fingertips to his forehead, as Noelle had seen him do at the campgrounds. First Sage softly chanted. Wise One copied the gesture and began to pray aloud as well. The two rocked together, in rhythm to their singing.

Hanover got up and stood in front of First Sage. "Answer me!" He slapped the devotee across the face. First Sage continued chanting. Noelle flinched; she hadn't expected Hanover to get so riled.

"Stop it!" Hanover shouted. "Stop this silliness! Tell me, where are the plans? Who is your buyer? How much is he paying you? What have you done with the payment?"

A thought jolted Noelle so hard she nearly fell off the chair. She recalled what Trevor had told her some days ago. To find out what SPARK was doing, he said, she had to *follow the money* . . .

Noelle stood up. "If I may interrupt." Hanover turned and glared at her. She ignored his angry look and instead gazed at First Sage, while speaking in a perfect Russian accent. "Comrade, tell us. Who handles the money for SPARK? Who collects the funds and pays the expenses for the devotees?"

Hanover opened his mouth to rebuke her, but Noelle held up a hand to stop him.

Wise One and First Sage stopped their chanting. First Sage smiled. At last, a question he could honestly answer. "Mac is our treasurer." He spoke matter of fact. "Mac takes care of our finances, leaving us free to pursue higher matters. He raises the funds we need to carry on our great work."

"Do you trust him?" she asked.

Wise One finally spoke. "Yes, implicitly."

"How long have you known him?"

"Quite a long while," said Wise One.

Noelle said, "What is his full name?"

Wise One giggled. "He has always been known to us as Mac. That is sufficient."

"And how does he raise these funds?"

"Many ways," said First Sage. "He solicits wealthy donors who approve of our cause. He mails requests to the many people who can only give small amounts. But one penny, when joined with other coins, creates many dollars."

"Do you know of any specific donors?"

First Sage shook his head wearily. "Such matters contaminate the soul. Mac has sole control over our earthly needs so we can explore the heavenly realm."

Hanover said, "Lieutenant, I must speak with you in private."

She took a deep breath and met his eyes. "Yes, major." She turned off the tape recorder.

Dash said to the guards, "Keep them here." He opened the door, and Noelle followed him into the hall.

The senior operative shut the door and dropped the accent, as well as his good nature. "What the devil is this all about?"

Noelle spoke in her normal voice as well. "We're been running down the wrong path. Mac is our man. He's Old Scratch." He glared at her. "No, it makes sense, listen. Mac sells government secrets and hides the payments by funneling the cash through SPARK. It's the cleanest laundry operation in town. Nobody would suspect that such clean-cut kids were supported by dirty money. When Old Scratch goes out to see his spy contacts, he tells First Sage he's meeting a donor. Nobody knows what Mac's doing with the money. If the police get wise, Wise One takes the rap while Mac escapes. Blossom, the girl who was murdered, saw some of his financial ledgers. Mac caught her reading it and killed her."

Hanover pondered for a moment. Noelle could see the wheels turning in his head.

"And one more thing," she added. "If we had Old Scratch here, he'd have dropped the innocent act from the start. A real agent would know that you knew who he was and not try to hide it."

"All right." Hanover was cool and levelheaded once more. "We'll have to shift into a new plan. Come with me."

Hanover reentered the room. Noelle followed and sat at her desk, unsure of what the senior control operative wanted her to do at this point.

"Well, well, comrades." Dash stood behind the targets and resumed his Russian accent. "We are willing to forget your little indiscretions—for now." He slapped both of them on their shoulders. "No hard feelings? But the motherland would like a full investigation into your finances. We have a feeling you may be, shall we say, putting aside a little for your own use. We will be in touch when we are ready to examine your books. You are free to go." He spoke to the guards, "Take them back to their cells. Delouse them with the bug spray. Make sure they get a good long rest before they travel."

The prisoners got on their feet and bowed to Hanover, thanking him profusely for his generosity. The guards prodded the two with their guns and marched them into the hall. When the door was shut, Hanover let out a sigh. His shoulders sagged with exhaustion. He lit yet another cigarette and stood by the desk, smoking with quick, anxious puffs.

"That's it?" Noelle removed her glasses and set them on the table. "You're just letting them go?"

His voice was hard. "Of course. They're innocents. SIAMESE does not persecute innocents."

"Everybody makes mistakes."

"Mistakes cost lives."

"You're acting as if this were my fault."

"It is. We should have slowed down and investigated the men before bringing them in. What happens if they tell others what happened here?"

"I'm sorry, but it seemed obvious to me. Wise One and First Sage were acting like they were hiding something."

"You can't judge by appearances."

"I'm sorry. But speaking of appearances, that was a mean crack about them having lice."

"Miss McNabb, I was talking in code. I told the agents to put radioactive spray on the men so we can track where they go. Hopefully the innocents will lead us to Mac, if indeed he is the man we want. 'Good long rest' meant we will sedate the targets before moving them."

"Sorry. I keep underestimating you cats."

"That's a mistake our enemies often make."

"So the mission isn't a failure?"

"Perhaps not. When I slapped the men on their shoulders, I planted a bugging device on each of them so we can hear their conversation. I predict they'll go to Mac and warn him about the audit. If Mac is indeed Old Scratch, he may panic and make a run for it. If not, then we're back to square one. It's possible the burglar had the SPARK pamphlet for no reason at all." Hanover stubbed out his cigarette in the ashtray. "But for now, an agent will drive you home. You can't be late for your day job."

"But I want to help—"

"Changes in your routine would arouse suspicions."

"What are you going to do about Wise One and First Sage? I mean, you won't—?" She left the answer hanging.

"Kill them? Of course not. I'll hypnotize the prisoners so that they'll forget what happened here. Then we'll put them to sleep and drop them off inside the campgrounds."

"By the time you get there, the gate to the camp will be locked."

Dash raised an eyebrow. "We can open it." He stuffed the cigarette carton into his shirt pocket.

She got on her feet. "Mr. Hanover?"

He turned. "Yes?"

"Did you have to slap First Sage so hard?"

He spoke with no emotion. "We do what we need to do."

As Hanover walked to the door, he reverted to the Boris persona. His posture, stride and attitude returned to that of the KGB agent. Noelle marveled at the transformation. He could teach her a few things about acting.

An agent came to escort her to the dressing room where she removed the Russian costume and washed the makeup off her face. After portraying both a hippie and a Russian spy in one day, she was happy to just be herself and slip into "normal" clothes: a sweater, pants, socks and shoes from the SIAMESE wardrobe department. Another agent drove her home in a company car with the usual tinted windows to prevent her from seeing out. However, the excitement of the day had taken a toll, and she napped during the ride to her house.

Noelle arrived at her house with only minutes to put out a bowl of cat chow for His Royal Highness and drive to the theme park; no time to stop and put on her own clothes. She arrived at the park and threw on her Winter Witch's green makeup and black costume. The evening dragged on forever. After a day of intrigue with the spy cats, acting in a silly musical sketch was a bore. Between the shows, Noelle stayed in the dressing room and tried to read a paperback romance novel, but she couldn't concentrate. She kept watching the wall clock, mentally urging the minute hand to move faster. Life in predictable, unremarkable Yuletide paled beside the life-and-death stakes of international espionage.

At long last, she took the group bow of the final show of the night. She tore down the backstage steps in record time, doffed the costume, gave her face a

204 Hippie Haven Homicide

fast wipe to remove some of the makeup—enough so she didn't look like a giant pea pod—tossed on her street clothes and left with a brief goodbye to her fellow cast members.

Noelle ignored their taunts of "What's the rush, Noelle? Got a hot date tonight?"

She longed to tell them, "I sure do—with a spy!"

As she got home, Noelle ignored Ceebee's pleas for attention and dialed the SIAMESE number on her Princess phone. She asked to be patched through to Destiny and hung up. After serving yet more kibble for the cat and making a late-night snack for herself—a chicken-salad sandwich with lettuce on white bread and a glass of milk—the phone rang.

"Black Manx calling Tabby Gray." Static on the line muffled the voice.

"Dest—I mean, Black Manx! Hi! Have the innocents gotten in touch with you-know-who?"

"I can't talk for long. I'm in the field. At this distance our radio batteries conk out. The innocents spent the evening praying with the devotees. Then they had a long, long discussion about company finances. But they finally went to the camp office and called the target to set up a meeting for tomorrow."

"Aren't they going to see him now?"

"This group hits the hay early. They'll be on the move after sunrise."

"Can I come along?"

"You may as well. Otherwise, you'll be hounding me every five minutes to see what's going on."

Destiny set a time to pick up Noelle and signed off. Noelle hung up the phone, quivering with anticipation. But what if Mac wasn't Old Scratch? Hanover wouldn't tolerate another goof from her. Other thoughts bothered her as she put on her pajamas. Did Cynthia Grizelda really not wish to see her niece? Was Dash lying about her aunt? If so, why? And what did he mean that SIAMESE was "illegal and clandestine?" Should she keep working for these people? Was she compromising her morals? Was she in too deep to get out? And why did Ceebee always have to hog the middle of the bed when she wanted to sleep?

Chapter 21: I Will Follow Him
Monday

The pair of headlights coming down the gravel drive must be Destiny's car. Noelle stepped away from her front window and turned off the porch light, as the sky would turn brighter in minutes. Noelle knew they'd be active today, so she had put on a thick turtleneck sweater to avoid a burdensome jacket, as well as pants and sneakers. She didn't want to mess with a purse, so after locking the front door she hid her house keys under a bush near the porch. Noelle still had some reservations about the dark side of SIAMESE she had seen creeping to the forefront recently. Perhaps this should be her last mission for the organization until she learned more about them.

Soon Noelle and Destiny were speeding to Holiday Acres. The rosy glow of dawn began to spread over the sky to welcome in a new day, a new week, new opportunities and dangers.

Destiny said. "I'll watch the Caddy. You keep your eyes on this." She pointed to a tiny radar dish set atop the car's dashboard. "It'll pick up the radioactive spray on their clothing."

"What if they changed clothes?"

Destiny shot her a glance. "Have you ever seen them wear anything else but those robes?"

At the gate of the campgrounds, Destiny parked on the shoulder of the road and waited until the security guard unlocked and pushed back the iron gate. A few minutes later, the SPARK Cadillac pulled out, with the chauffeur in front and Wise One and First Sage in the back seat. The radar dish beeped and spun to face the vehicle. Destiny followed the Caddy at a distance.

"Are we going to listen in on their microphones?" Noelle asked.

"Maybe later," Destiny replied. "They won't be saying much in front of their driver."

"What if they spot us?"

"They won't. If they're innocents, they won't expect someone on their tail." Destiny glanced in the rear-view mirror. "We, on the other hand, have a visitor." Noelle started to turn around to look through the back window. "No, don't peek. They were waiting further up the road."

"Is it the wild card?"

"Probably. They got the same idea we did: follow the head cheese to the money man."

"How did they find out about Mac?"

"Everyone's got their own way of doing spycraft."

"Maybe they followed us."

Destiny shot her a dark look. "No, they didn't."

The Caddy took the on-ramp to the highway going south toward Riverbend. Destiny and the shadow followed. Destiny tailed the Caddy for a while, then sped up and passed the car in the left lane. The shadow did the same, settling in between the SIAMESE car and the Caddy. Destiny changed lanes again and slowed, allowing both cars to pass. Then she settled back in behind the Caddy. The shadow car shifted lanes and waited for Destiny to pass, once more moving behind her back bumper.

"I was right," said Destiny. "Our pal is playing leapfrog with us."

"We better shake them," said Noelle.

"Not yet. If we get off the highway, we'll lose the target. We'll wait until we're in town."

The Caddy passed the first exit into Riverbend and the second. Was the car planning to bypass the city altogether and cross the bridge into Kentucky? Just before reaching the Ohio River, though, the

SPARK car left the highway and headed into the downtown area. The narrow one-way streets lined with parked cars along the curbs made driving even more challenging. An air of neglect hung over the area, as consumers had neglected the older, smaller stores to shop at the exciting new offerings at the Raintree Mall and the suburban shopping centers. The Caddy made several turns onto various streets.

"Keep your eye on the radar," Destiny ordered. "They know we're here."

The trio of cars drove onto a residential street lined with three-story brick apartment buildings as well as two-story vintage houses, each one now cut up into multiple housing units. The sidewalks were empty, as were the roads. The shadow car pulled closed and tapped the back bumper of the SIAMESE car. After a moment it rammed again, harder.

Noelle twisted around to look out the rear window. "He's trying to push us off the road!"

"I'm not in the mood for a fight or a surrender." Destiny waited until the Caddy turned left onto another street. She kept going straight. "Time to ditch our friend." She pressed a button on the dashboard. From a box inside the center of the back window shot a beam of light. The bright ray shone into the eyes of the shadow driver. Blinded, the driver slammed on his brakes and swerved. He crashed into a parked car with the crunch of shattered metal. Destiny sped away and turned right at the intersection.

"But the Caddy went left," Noelle said.

"Yeah, I know. I wanted to fool our shadow once he gets his sight back. Watch the radar and tell me where to go."

Her eyes locked on the radar device, Noelle gave directions and Destiny maneuvered around the streets until they were, once again, behind the target—but they had lost the shadow.

Eventually the Caddy stopped in a parking lot along the Ohio River. The smell of river water permeated the air. Overhead some birds flew in the clear sky. The temperature was slightly cooler than inland. Small motorboats, for use by private citizens in their leisure, were tied up along the dock. Workers loaded cargo onto small shipping vessels. Otherwise, the shoreline was quiet and calm. Riverbend was a small port, not a huge commercial center like Louisville to the east or St. Louis to the west, so it saw minimal river traffic.

The chauffeur got out of the Cadillac and opened the back door for Wise One and First Sage to exit. Destiny stopped the car behind a row of parked cars. The chauffer got back in the Caddy to wait as Wise One and First Sage entered a small, dingy restaurant. The run-down building had peeling paint and large windows overlooking the water.

"A funny place for a meeting," said Noelle.

"Not if you're planning a quick escape. My gut tells me once they talk to Mac, he won't hang around for long."

Destiny opened the lid of a compartment wedged between the two front seats. She removed a telephone receiver attached to long cord connected to radio installed in the car. "Black Manx to kennel," the code name for SIAMESE headquarters. "Emergency need for aquatic transport at river's edge. Anticipate fugitive in flight." She put the phone back into its holder. "Now we turn on the microphones and find out how soon our rat plans to leave his sinking ship."

Destiny switched off the radar tracker and flipped a toggle on the dashboard, activating the mics that

Hanover had planted on the devotees' robes. Voices, weak but audible, came across a small speaker embedded in the dashboard. The women listened to some small talk with a bored waitress as she seated the pair "in a corner," as First Sage had requested.

"Wouldn't you rather sit here by the window with a view?" she asked.

"No, thank you." First Sage then ordered two cups of hot herbal tea.

A nondescript black car pulled into a parking spot close to the restaurant. A lone man with a thick crop of red hair exited the car. Noelle's heart thumped. Was this the man who had rented a rowboat on the day that Blossom died? Was he a spy, a traitor and a murderer all rolled into one? The man entered the restaurant. A new voice was overheard over the car speaker, ordering coffee.

"He obviously isn't a devotee," said Noelle. "They don't drink coffee."

Destiny hushed her.

"Thank you for meeting with us on such short notice, Mac," said First Sage. "But why did you wish to come to such an out-of-the-way place? We have plenty of space at the campgrounds."

"Yuletide's out of my way." The new voice was deep, husky and clipped. "I have business to do in Riverbend. I've lined up appointments for some potential new donors, so I can't stay here long. Last night you mentioned something about an audit."

The word "audit" triggered the post-hypnotic suggestion that Hanover had planted. First Sage spoke mechanically, according to the instructions Dash had given him. "Yes. An audit. The IRS has questions about our finances."

"I see no need for an audit," said Mac. "Our books are clean. I've always been above board with SPARK. Haven't I, Wise One?"

"Oh, yes, yes indeed," said the childlike voice. "I am pleased with your work for us. But the government, that is another matter. They are suspicious when a simple group like ours comes into much money. That is their nature. I do not blame them. Money can be a temptation and the cause of many deceptions."

"Yes, of course." Mac spoke quickly. "I assure you that SPARK has no cause for concern. But I'll do what you want. How soon do you need the information?"

"Soon, very soon," said First Sage.

"I need some time to get the books. Naturally I don't carry the information on me."

"But of course. Also, the IRS wants a list of our donors."

"Really? Why?" Mac's voice changed its tone, as if he were getting suspicious.

"They need to verify names and addresses so they can weed out any false accounts," said First Sage. "You understand."

"Indeed, I do." Over the speaker came a loud slurp of coffee. Mac's tone changed to overly friendly. "Tell me what happened yesterday at the rally."

First Sage replied. "We were seated on the bandstand. Some men kidnapped the Wise One and myself. We escaped and returned to the campgrounds. There is much evil in the world, even in a place like Yuletide."

"Kidnap?" Mac's tone turned ugly. "What did the men look like?"

212 Hippie Haven Homicide

First Sage followed his post-hypnotic orders. "They were masked. Yes, they wore black masks."

"Where did they take you?"

"To a dark room."

"How did the two of you manage to overpower these men?"

Wise One broke in. "The power of goodness and right will always overcome the wickedness that taints our mortal existence."

"I see." Mac didn't sound convinced.

Destiny switched off the speaker. "He's onto us. He knows those two couldn't possibly beat up a gang of hoods." She picked up the phone receiver. "Black Manx calling kennel. Is the aquatic transport ready?"

"Affirmative," came the reply.

"Roger. We're on the move." She put away the receiver, closed the container, and opened her door. "Come on."

"Aren't we going to follow Mac?"

"We are, but not by car."

Destiny hoofed it to the walkway that lined the waterfront. Noelle hustled to catch up with her. The women stayed clear of the restaurant's windows so the men inside wouldn't see them.

Destiny handed Noelle the radio comb. "You stay here and follow Mac when he leaves the building. See which boat he gets on and call me. I'll be on our boat—the *Cat's Paw*—at the end of the riverfront. If you want to ride along, you'll have to boogie. As soon as you call, we'll be scooting. Mac won't wait for us."

"Got it." Noelle tucked the comb into a pants pocket. "SIAMESE has a boat?"

"I'd rather have the minisub, but another agent is using it. And don't let Mac spot you." Destiny ran down the walkway to prepare the *Cat's Paw* for launch.

Noelle needed a way to look inconspicuous as she waited for Mac. Just staring at the restaurant door looked too obvious. If she had brought her purse, she could at least powder her nose. A fishing store was nearby, so she gazed at the display window and feigned an interest in the rods, reels, nets and lures.

"Hey! Hey you!" A burly man poked his head out of the shop door.

"Who, me?" said Noelle.

"You've been gawking at my stuff for five minutes. Are you buying or not?"

"Sorry. Just browsing."

"Then move along so the paying customers can come inside." He ducked back inside the store.

Arguing would attract unwanted attention, so Noelle sauntered slowly down the pier, glancing over her shoulder at the greasy spoon. A man and women left together. At last Mac left the restaurant, heading toward her. Noelle bent over and retied her shoes. After he passed by, she straightened up and spoke into the comb radio.

"Tabby Gray to Black Manx. Target on the move, going west."

"Roger," Destiny replied.

Mac hurried down the pier, but the walkway was lightly populated and Noelle had no trouble following him from a distance. Halfway down the dock, he stopped and untied the mooring ropes of a small motorboat with the name *Tranquility* stenciled on the side. Noelle quickened her pace. Once she passed the boat she radioed again.

"Tabby Gray here. He's aboard a black boat called the *Tranquility*."

"Good. Get your tail down here PDQ. Last boat on the pier."

Noelle glanced back. Mac had started the engine. The propeller churned the water. She tore into a run. By the time she reached the end of the walkway, the *Cat's Paw* had its engines roaring. The boat drifted from the pier.

Destiny, standing aft, held out her hands to catch Noelle. "Jump!"

Noelle ran toward the boat and gathered her strength for one mighty leap. At the end of the dock, she sprang over the water. Destiny leaned over the edge of the boat and grabbed Noelle's wrists just as she began to fall. She pulled as Noelle scrambled for a foothold on the side of the slippery boat. The *Cat's Paw* sped away from the shore. A spray of water hit Noelle as she climbed onto the deck. She shook the water off her arms, grateful for the warmth of the sweater.

Noelle pointed at the *Tranquility* as it headed into open water. "There he is!"

Destiny stood beside the pilot, another SIAMESE agent. Two other men stood on the deck near the stern, their eyes hidden behind sunglasses, not only to hide their identities but also to protect their eyes against the glare of the sun on the water. Destiny didn't take time to introduce the men to Noelle because everyone was focused on the speedboat, which zipped along surprisingly fast.

"He must have some kind of modified engine to move like that." Noelle had to shout to be heard over the roar of the *Cat's Paw*'s motor.

"So do we," Destiny replied.

The river had little boat traffic, which gave the *Tranquility* plenty of space to zig and zag in an effort to escape. The bow of the *Cat's Paw* tipped up and sliced through the murky river water. Noelle hadn't spent much time in motorboats, and she lacked sea legs. She grabbed the deck railing with both hands to keep from falling. Her stomach couldn't keep up with the sharp turns, and she regretted eating a large breakfast. The cold air reddened her cheeks. The *Cat's Paw* poured on more horsepower as it strived to keep up with its prey. The SIAMESE boat had a bigger engine, but the smaller *Tranquility* could outmaneuver its pursuer. The *Cat's Paw* swung wide to close in front of the *Tranquility* and cut it off. In response, Mac made a sharp turn and sped back the way he came.

The *Cat's Paw* drew closer. Destiny picked up a bullhorn. "*Cat's Paw* calling *Tranquility*. Stop and prepare for boarding."

Mac glanced over his shoulder and revved up his boat even faster.

The *Cat's Paw* pilot shouted, "We're top speed. If he goes any faster, we'll burn the engines."

"What kind of jazzed-up boat does he have?" Destiny said. "I've never seen anyone tear along like that. Prepare the hook."

Another agent stepped up and opened a panel in the dashboard, revealing a series of switches and buttons. He pressed a red button and a three-prong grappling hook attached to a long line shot out of the bow. Noelle gasped. The boat was armed? But why should she expect anything less from SIAMESE. The hook came close to snagging the *Tranquility*, but the more agile boat swerved and the hook fell into the water.

Mac's boat darted to and fro in the water, creating a hard-to-hit moving target. Destiny ordered the agent to retrieve the hook, and a crank reeled in the line and hook. Mac turned his boat full around and raced to ram head on into the *Cat's Paw*'s bow. Mac closed in. At the last minute, Destiny ordered a hard left to evade the oncoming boat. The sudden turn caught Noelle off balance. The railing was too wet for her to hold on. Her sneakers lost their footing on the damp deck and her feet slid out from under her. She fell and rolled under the metal railing—right into the river.

Noelle caught her breath and closed her eyes just as she plunged into the dark water. She didn't panic. As a kid Noelle had taken swimming classes at the Yuletide city pool, and she'd aced her Girl Scout swimming badge. Noelle opened her eyes and the dirty water stung her eyeballs. Her muscles contracted with the shock of the cold water. She kicked hard and pushed with her arms to reach the surface. Her knit sweater soaked up the water, and the increasing weight slowed her down. At last, her head broke through the surface and she gasped the air, treading water the best she could in the clunky shoes.

"Help! Help! Girl overboard!" she screamed.

The water in her eyes blurred her vision. She could see some indistinct boat hulls. Should she swim to shore or wait for someone to pick her up? Noelle swallowed the nasty-tasting water and spat it out just as a boat pulled up beside her and lowered a rope ladder. Tired but grateful, she grabbed the ladder and scrambled up. How nice for a Good Samaritan to rescue her. Up on the deck, she wiped the water out of her eyes and tried to catch her breath.

"Thanks a lot! I really appreciate—"

Mac, standing on the deck, scowled at her.

She'd boarded the wrong boat.

Chapter 22: Heroes And Villains

Mac was average height, but built stocky. He looked like someone who could throw a nasty punch with no hesitation. His puffy black jacket was zipped to the neck. He had on black pants and black gloves. Although he was in his thirties, deep creases lined his suntanned face. His hands were large enough to strangle someone. His black eyes had no soul in them. A chill ran over Noelle, more from fear than a chill. She turned to jump back into the river, willing to risk another dunking than to deal with the enemy. Mac grabbed her arms and threw her onto one of the metal chairs bolted to the deck.

"Who are you?" he yelled over the roar of the motor. The autopilot switch kept the boat at a standstill. "The CIA?"

"No. Not CIA."

"Who, then?"

"I don't rat on my friends."

He slapped Noelle across the face. His onyx ring cut into her skin. Pain shot through her face, and blood trickled down her cheek. Noelle was too dazed and weary to fight Mac as he slapped handcuffs around her wrists and ankles. Mac released the autopilot and continued his flight down the river. He ramped up the speed, and the *Cat's Paw* fell back.

"Are you going to kill me?" she shouted.

Mac kept his eyes ahead as he steered. "After I make you talk. But not here. Bodies float. I have a safer place for disposal." He talked as if he were discussing taking out a bag of household trash.

"Were you inside the camper with First Sage and Wise One at the Riverbend rally?"

He turned to her, a quizzical look on his face. Mac's eyes burned like coals.

Noelle continued. "My friends and I taped that conversation. We heard two voices, but there had to be a third person in there."

He put his eyes back on the open water. "I was eating lunch. I stay out of the conversation when the other two yak."

"And you were the one who killed Trevor's story about the dead girl at the *Yuletide Herald*."

"I handle the press for the organization."

"Why did you kill Blossom?" she said.

Mac shot her another quick glance. "Who?"

"The girl devotee. The one who died at the campground. You made it look like a drug overdose."

"Are you nuts? I'd never kill one of the kids. They're harmless, and I can't afford to lose my position with SPARK."

"I think you murdered Blossom because she saw the file that said you were stealing money from the Wise One."

"She wasn't going to blab. I tell people to keep their yaps shut and they do."

"Then who killed her?"

"Shut up!"

Cat's Paw was far behind *Tranquility*. At this rate, Mac would soon escape to his hiding place, wherever that was. But he began slowing the *Tranquility* so the other boat could catch up. Why would he want to lose such an advantage? Mac reset the autopilot and headed aft. A tarp covered an object on the deck. He tore off the covering and revealed a machine gun. Noelle gasped. With the weapon, Mac could not only sink the *Cat's Paw* but also kill everyone aboard. If SIAMESE fired back, Noelle would be hit by friendly fire. Not a pleasant prospect.

Noelle struggled against the boat's rocking to get on her feet. Mac had his back to her as he prepared the gun, so he didn't see her. With her feet hobbled, Noelle took a small hop. Good. She landed on her feet. With the engine noise and lapping of the water, Mac didn't hear her move. She jumped again, getting closer. On the third leap, she landed on top of Mac and knocked him down.

As Mac landed on the deck, his jacket scooted up, uncovering a gun tucked into his pants. Noelle grabbed the gun, and rolled away from him, landing on her stomach. Mac scrambled to his feet. Noelle gripped the gun with both hands, held her arms straight out and, with her finger glued to the trigger, emptied the bullet cartridge into the engine. Cursing, Mac leaned over and wrestled the gun away.

A plume of smoke rose from the dead motor, oil spilled onto the deck, and the boat stopped. Mac straightened up and fired at Noelle, but the gun had run out of ammo. Fire broke out on the boat and the hull abruptly tilted. The air turned foul with the stench of spilled gasoline leaking into the water. Mac dropped the gun and jumped over the side, swiftly swimming away.

Noelle grabbed one of the deck chairs and struggled to her feet. What a choice—stay on the ship and be burned alive, or take another dip into the river and drown. With her hands and feet bound she had little hope of swimming, but at least a drowned corpse would look nicer for a funeral than one charred by flames. Her mind was quickly made up when the engine exploded and the force knocked Noelle into the river. The water felt even colder this time. She couldn't move her feet to tread water and she sank. Noelle mentally sent off a prayer, ready to meet her Lord and Savior in the afterlife.

Noelle began rising out of the water. She heard a voice. An angel? God welcoming her into heaven?

"Breathe! Breathe!" Destiny yanked Noelle's head out of the water and turned her partner onto her back. When the spy had seen the *Tranquility* sinking, she surmised that Noelle was in danger, and she dove into the river.

"Just float. Float! Don't fight me. I got you. Relax and breathe, you silly girl!"

With one arm around Noelle, Destiny swam with strong strokes back to the *Cat's Paw*. Upon reaching the boat, which had come to a full stop, another agent dropped a rope that Destiny tied around Noelle's waist. The agents on deck pulled the soggy swimmer aboard. They set her on the molded plastic bench that ran along the port side of the boat. An agent wrapped a blanket around Noelle's shaking shoulders. Her arms and legs trembled from the cold water.

Destiny was soon seated beside her. "How are you feeling? You still with us?"

Noelle nodded, too exhausted to talk. She held out her hands, a pleading look in her eyes. Destiny removed a hairpin from her afro and picked the locks of the 'cuffs, freeing her partner's hands and feet. A commotion starboard caught the women's attention. The agents were operating a crane that had dropped a large rope net over the side of the boat. The crane pulled up the netting and dropped its contents onto the deck.

Destiny walked over to the net. "We got us the blue-ribbon prize catch today."

Inside the net, Mac clawed at the ropes and struggled to get out. The agents extracted Mac from the netting and used Noelle's handcuffs to bind the enemy's wrists behind his back. Destiny ordered the agents to take Mac below deck. The pilot revved up the boat and headed back to shore. Destiny fetched the first aid kit and put some iodine and a Band-Aid on Noelle's face cut. The spy also found a thermos of steaming hot coffee, which she poured into a plastic cup and offered to Noelle, who gratefully slurped down the coffee. Destiny sat beside Noelle as she described her adventure aboard the *Tranquility*.

"It's a shame you crippled the boat," said Destiny. "SIAMESE could use a motor like that. We're fighting with horse and buggies when the enemy uses rocket ships. Why didn't you shoot Mac and leave the boat intact?"

"Oh, Destiny," said Noelle. "You know I can't kill anyone. Goes against my morals."

"Someday those morals are going to kill you."

"Yeah, but at least I'll have a clean conscience when I reach the Pearly Gates. Say, what's going to happen when Old Scratch goes on trial? If I have to give testimony in court, I'll blow my cover."

Destiny turned her face away from Noelle as she packed away the first aid kit. She spoke with no emotion. "We won't need you. SIAMESE will take care of Mac."

An uneasy feeling crept over Noelle. "Are you going to kill him?"

"You stay here and rest. I'm going to talk to the prisoner."

On that note, Destiny went below deck, leaving Noelle alone to dry off in the sun and worry over the principles and actions of the ruthless agents of SIAMESE.

After the boat docked, one of the agents drove Noelle home. Destiny and the other agents bundled Mac into a van and headed for SIAMESE headquarters. During the drive, Noelle felt the nagging itch of unfinished business. Old Scratch had said he didn't murder Blossom. He had no reason to lie to Noelle, since he had planned to kill her. And if

Mac had felt Blossom was a threat to his money scheme, he would have bumped her off long ago when she had seen the files and not waited for weeks to pass. But if not Mac, then who murdered the girl?

Chapter 23: I'll Get You

As Noelle walked into her cottage, the phone rang. She was tempted to ignore it and let the person call back, but SIAMESE might have some news about the mission. Noelle picked up the phone, but instead of Hanover or Destiny, she had Julia on the line.

"I looked for you at church yesterday, but I didn't see you," Julie said. "I wanted to tell you all about my shopping spree."

"Yeah, I'm sorry I missed it." Noelle was too drained to think up a plausible excuse for her absence. "Just wasn't feeling well, I guess."

"That's too bad. I gotta tell you, we found the cutest dresses—"

"Julia, I'm sure the clothes are nice, but can you call me back later? I need to get some rest. I'd love to hear all about it when I'm feeling better."

"It's so hard to get a hold of you these days. I think you're trying to avoid me."

Noelle had been letting the spy work get the bulk of her attention. Now that Old Scratch was safely out of the way, she should spend some time with her Yuletide life. Maybe the SIAMESE cats didn't have friends or family, but she did.

"Tell you what, Julia. Let me take a nap. Then I can come over to your house later and we can gab."

"Oh, Noelle, that sounds wonderful! Why don't you drop by for supper? Then I can show you the fabric swatches and everything!"

Noelle then called her mom and took a rain check on the usual Monday night family dinner. Julia would appreciate the time she was willing to spend with her, and besides, Julia's mother could whip up a pretty good meal.

After a bath, a short nap and a light lunch, Noelle felt her usual perky self again. She had one more task to do before her girl's night with Julia. She put on a sweater, midi-skirt and knee boots. She called Trevor at his home and told him to come with her to the campgrounds for "the scoop of the century." Noelle picked up the reporter as he was waiting outside his apartment building and headed for Holiday Acres, arriving just in time. The devotees had packed up their meager belongings and were ready to leave town. Noelle and Trevor found the followers gathered in the dining hall, snacking on pastries, fruit tarts, cookies and fried dough sticks topped with cinnamon, all set out on a long table. The urn with Blossom's ashes sat on a smaller table. Chakra told the visitors that the group was going to leave as soon as one of Blossom's family members arrived to take the ashes home. Noelle and Trevor then asked Wise One and First Sage to speak with them privately. The foursome retreated to one of the cabins. Noelle and Trevor sat on one bunk and the two devotees perched on the edge of another bed facing them.

"I'm afraid I have bad news for you," said Noelle. "Mac, the man who handled the SPARK money, is really a dangerous spy who used the code name Old Scratch. He funded your operation with money he earned by selling government secrets to foreign interests. A big chunk of the money he kept for himself."

"No, no, this cannot be true," said First Sage.

Wise One held up a hand. "Be still and hear her out."

Noelle continued as Trevor took shorthand notes in his notebook. "Right after Mac met with the two of you this morning, he tried to leave town on a motorboat. He had no intention of turning over the financial records, at least not the real ones. He wasn't going to talk to any donors, as he told you. During the chase, Mac tried to kill the people chasing him with a machine gun set up on his boat. Federal agents have him now for questioning."

Noelle omitted her own involvement with the incident. And she lied about SIAMESE agents. They had no connection with federal agencies, but trying to explain the clandestine group would prove too cumbersome—especially since Noelle didn't understand it herself.

Trevor stopped writing and looked at Noelle. "How do you know this?"

"I'll tell you later." Which Noelle had no intention of doing.

"There must be a simple explanation," said First Sage. "We must speak with Mac and hear his side of the story."

"That won't be possible," said Noelle. "Mac won't be coming back to you. He's . . . he's in federal custody."

Wise One cried. He took a square of colored silk from inside his robe and sobbed into it.

"I'm sorry," said Noelle. "I didn't mean to upset anyone. But you needed to know the truth."

"Indeed, yes," said Wise One. "I thank you for that. I see that you are an honest girl. I was so eager to spread my message of love that I made a deal with the devil to provide the money I needed. Shame on me. I am a fool."

"No, Wise One, don't be sad," said Noelle. "It isn't your fault. Mac could have fooled anyone."

"Was Mac the one who put the kibosh on my story?" Trevor asked.

"Yes." Noelle then addressed First Sage. "Did Mac tell the *Herald* not to run a story about Blossom's death?"

"I do not know," said First Sage. "We allowed Mac to intercede for us with the media. We trusted him implicitly. We never checked on what he was doing. That was our mistake. I apologize if he caused you any hardship. It was never our intention to keep our actions a secret."

A big smile creased Trevor's face. "Of course, you realize that with Mac not here to blindside the publishers, this story will go out. Just think, Noelle, my story might be syndicated nationwide!"

Noelle frowned at him. "Don't be greedy. That's what got Mac into trouble."

"This is very bad," said First Sage. "If you have any mercy, please don't publish this. SPARK will lose credibility. People will assume we are criminals. The police may arrest the devotees."

Noelle eyed Trevor. "Your story will state that Wise One and First Sage were never involved in any criminal activities, and that Mac alone is the bad guy. All of the devotees are in the clear. Right?"

Trevor glowered at her. "Everyone's an editor."

"She is correct," said Wise One. "Honesty is always the right path. We must show the world that we are willing to admit our mistakes, no matter how painful. Confession is the first step toward healing."

"What of our money?" said First Sage. "We know nothing about what Mac has done with our funds or how to get to them. What of our property in St. Louis? Does it belong to us or to Mac? We must still feed and shelter the children. If our monies are hidden, we may have nothing and no place to go."

"I know some lawyers in town," said Trevor. "And they know accountants in Riverbend who can sort out your finances. If you're desperate, one of the banks in town may be able to float you a loan until you're back on your feet."

"You are so kind," said Wise One. "And so complex. You give both bad news and helpful advice at the same time."

A devotee walked into the cabin and bowed. "A thousand pardons for interrupting, Wise One, but the pagan is here to collect the mortal remains of our sister."

"Ah, yes. I'll take care of it," said First Sage. "If you'll excuse me, Wise one."

"No, no, I must be present to see that our sister is safely transported away," said Wise One.

"If you don't mind, I'd like to come long," said Noelle. "I feel terrible that we haven't found Blossom's killer. I can at least say goodbye to her."

"Let's all go." Trevor tucked his pen and notebook into the inside pocket of his sports coat. "I think we're finished here."

The devotee led the group into the dining room. The table goodies caught Noelle's eye. She loved sweets, and maybe she could grab a bite before leaving. As she was looking over the snacks, First Sage addressed someone standing behind her.

"Before you return home on the bus," said First Sage, "please, help yourself to our desserts. They have been blessed and prepared with love."

An unfamiliar voice said, "Naw, I can't eat sugar. I'm diabetic."

Noelle turned and stared at the speaker. A dozen stray thoughts fell in place. Her mind felt like a Vegas slot machines that had hit the jackpot.

She blurted to the red-haired man, "Why did you kill Blossom?"

A flush ran over the man's cheeks, highlighting his freckles. His mouth gaped. "I—what? You're crazy!"

"What are you saying?" said Wise One. "This is Jeb Thomas. He is Blossom's brother."

Noelle said to Jeb, "You rented a rowboat the day Blossom died. You rowed into camp and left a note in Blossom's cabin, telling her to meet you. She trusted you, so she came down to the fire pit."

"Who is this broad?" said Jeb. "She's wacky!"

Noelle continued. "You tried to convince Blossom to return to Homestead with you. When she wouldn't leave, you killed her. Then you jabbed one of your empty insulin needles into her arm to make it look like a drug overdose. But you also left this." Noelle took a dirty strip of paper from her purse. "I found this at a fire pit a couple of days after her death. I finally looked at it today. It's a one-way bus ticket from Yuletide to Homestead. You brought the ticket with you so you could take Blossom back to Illinois with you."

"You're a goofhead!" the man yelled. "You're all a bunch of goofheads!"

First Sage grabbed Jeb by his shoulder and looked him in the eye. "This woman has been truthful with us on other matters. Now tell us, swearing on whatever you hold sacred, did you kill your dear sister?"

"STEP sister!" Jeb bellowed. "Stepsister! She ain't my real sister! My mom didn't have Janet! I hated her!" He grabbed First Sage's wrists and pushed him to the floor. Jeb raced out of the dining room.

"Get him!" Noelle shouted.

The male devotees fled the building after the fugitive. They gathered up their robes around their knees and, with wads of fabric clutched in their fists, ran after Jeb. Their hairy, white legs were thin but strong. Jeb was fast, but the devotees were determined, and they knew the campgrounds better. Jeb raced down the concrete walkway that led to the parking lot. Half of the devotees took a shortcut, a dirt path that wound through the woods. They reached the parking lot ahead of Jeb. The rest of the devotees clustered behind Jeb to stop him from backtracking. The killer was trapped between the two groups. The men grabbed Jeb's arms and dragged him, kicking and yelling, back to the dining room. They placed in him a chair and circled around him to prevent another escape.

"Can you guys hold him?" said Trevor. "I'll go and call the cops." He raced to the office to use the phone.

First Sage stood before the accused killer. "Now will you confess and clear your soul of its wickedness?"

"All right, all right." Jeb was angry and not at all repentant. "I was glad to see Janet leave home. She was a pest. But my mom loved picking on Janet and, with her gone, mom got on my case all the time. I thought if Janet was home, mom would leave me alone. I rode the bus to this dippy town to get my stepsister, but the stupid girl wanted to stay with you lame bunch of goonies. I showed Janet the bus ticket and she threw it away. She got stubborn and hit me. She's one mean little fighter. I pushed her back. She tripped and conked her head. Wasn't my fault. If she'd been nice and left without fussing, she'd still be alive."

"Indeed, yes," said Wise One, "But she would feel dead inside."

Yuletide's one and only squad car arrived. The police chief wasn't among the officers who arrived, so Noelle was spared Whitlock's cutting remarks about her playing amateur sleuth. The police took Jeb into custody. First Sage ordered the devotees to pack up the treats and clean up the dining hall so they could depart. Wise One decided to take Blossom's urn with them for burial at a suitable place.

Noelle said to First Sage, "Where are you going? Another rally at another town?"

"I do not know," said First Sage. "We had plans. But that has changed. Wise One will need to direct us."

"If you'll permit me," said Noelle, "I have an idea. SPARK needs a reliable—and honest—source of income. You can't depend on others to pay your bills. And your devotees should do something more productive besides playing ball in the park. Why don't you set up a farm here in southern Indiana? There's plenty of rich farmland. You can raise your own food and keep dairy cattle. You can make honey and jellies and crafts to sell. You might even run a shop inside the theme park. Your wares would be a smash hit with the tourists."

First Sage turned to Wise One. "That sounds most wise. Perhaps pagans do have some insights worthy to share with us."

Wiser One nodded. "Yes, indeed. We shall break with our troubled past and begin anew. We will settle here among the good folk of Yuletide and work hard. Blessings on you, Miss McNabb, for opening the eyes of an old man who is just now beginning to see clearly."

Noelle smiled. "God brought us together for a reason. And I like your spirit. I believe you're sincere in what you're doing for your followers. All you needed was a spark of faith."

THE END

ABOUT THE AUTHOR

 Sally Carpenter is a native Hoosier now living in Moorpark, California.

Book One in the Psychedelic Spy series is *Flower Power Fatality*.

Sally also pens the Sandy Fairfax Teen Idol Series, also with Cozy Cat Press: *The Baffled Beatlemaniac Caper (*2012 Eureka! Award finalist for best first mystery novel)*, The Sinister Sitcom Caper*, *The Cunning Cruise Ship Caper* and *The Quirky Quiz Show Caper*.

She wrote a Sandy Fairfax short story, "The Puzzling Puppet Show Caper," for the CCP anthology, *Cozy Cat Shorts*, and Chapter Three for the CCP group mystery *Chasing the Codex*.

She has stories in two other anthologies: "Dark Nights at the Deluxe Drive-in" for *Last Exit to Murder* and "Faster Than a Speeding Bullet" in *Plan B: Omnibus*.

Sally has a master's degree in theater from Indiana State University. While in school, her plays "Star Collector" and "Common Ground" were finalists in the American College Theater Festival One-Act Playwriting Competition. "Common Ground" also won a college creative writing award. "Star Collector" was produced in New York City and served as the inspiration for the Sandy Fairfax series.

She also has a Master of Divinity and a black belt in tae kwon do.

Reach Sally on Facebook. To download a free story, go to her webpage at: http://sandyfairfax.com.